Twilight Manors in Palm Springs
The Strange Case of Donna Reed's Missing Wig

A Brian & Stéphane Adventure

ST SUKIE DE LA CROIX

RATTLING GOOD YARNS
—— PRESS ——

Rattling Good Yarns Press
33490 Date Palm Drive 3065
Cathedral City CA 92235
USA
www.rattlinggoodyarns.com

Cover Design: Rattling Good Yarns Press

Library of Congress Control Number: 2022942655
ISBN: 978-1-955826-21-1

First Edition

Also by St Sukie de la Croix

Fiction

Twilight Manors in Palm Springs God's Waiting Room (Book 1)

The Orange Spong and Story Telling at the Vamp-Art Café

The Blue Spong and the Flight from Mediocrity

St Sukie's Strange Garden of Woodland Creatures (Illustrated by Roy
Alton Wald)

The Memoir of a Groucho Marxist: A Very British Fairy Tale

Nonfiction

*Last Call Chicago: A History of 1001 LGBTQ-Friendly Taverns, Haunts
& Hangouts,* with Rick Karlin

*Chicago After Stonewall: A History of LGBTQ Chicago From Gay Lib to
Gay Life*

*Out of the Underground: Homosexuals, The Radical Press, and the Rise and
Fall of the Gay Liberation Front*

Tell Me About It: LGBTQ Secrets, Confessions, and Life Stories, with
Owen Keehnen

Tell Me About It 2, with Owen Keehnen

Tell Me About It 3, with Owen Keehnen

Chicago Whispers: A History of LGBT Chicago Before Stonewall

To Martin Prime

"There comes a time in every woman's life when the only thing that helps is a glass of champagne."
– Bette Davis

1

Bleach

Stéphane Dobson and Brian McCartney had relocated from Chicago to Palm Springs a few months earlier. They moved into 49100 Las Pensamiento Rosados in a gated community for seniors called Puesta De Sol—known locally as Twilight Manors. Moving from fast-paced Chicago with its drive-by shootings and ball-freezing winters and then adjusting to the laidback California lifestyle had been fraught with problems. Stéphane and Brian were not the laidback types. In fact, they were the opposite. They were the storm in a teacup type. They were the big fuss about nothing type. In fact, they couldn't attend an ice cream social without it turning into a food fight—or a bloodbath. Brian had once slapped the mayor's wife in the face with a hymnal in Our Lady of Guadalupe Church. Stéphane fed bananas through a glory hole to their lascivious neighbor. And then there was the murdered nun they found in a thrift store.

Palm Springs is heaven on Earth. It's a great place to live, but an even better place to die. On warm summer evenings, when there's a cool breeze, all that can be heard is the flapping of rainbow flags, the clinking of cocktail glasses, and the squeaking of knees waiting to be replaced. Even the straight people in Palm Springs are a shade of lavender: the men, bearded, tattooed, and a tad limp-wristed; the women, sporting lesbian hair and golf shoes. Palm Springs airport is like a black hole in space; every plane that lands there enters a vortex of gay serenity. When a plane lands at Palm Springs airport, life itself shudders to a halt, and passengers disembark into a paradise of peace and quiet, sunshine, and a sea of seniors thumbing-through beaten-up copies of *People* magazine in God's Waiting Room. Chicago is so cold it can freeze your heart. Palm Springs can thaw it out and make an appointment for coronary artery bypass surgery in the blink of an eye.

Brian tightened the tie around his neck. He wasn't a "tie" person, more the Hawaiian shirt kind of person. In fact, he collected them, much to Stéphane's chagrin—Stéphane hated them. Even when Brian was teaching history at the University of Chicago, he never wore a tie. He only had two ties in his closet, both black and worn only for funerals and weddings. Of course, there are a lot of funerals in Palm Springs where death is as common as outbreaks of syphilis. They had already lost Larry, a nonagenarian neighbor with an abundance of genitals, who was buried in his favorite knock-off Oscar de la Renta green polka-dot bikini. But Stéphane and Brian were particularly saddened by the latest friend to pass away; and by the method of his passing. Yet again, death had cast a shadow over Twilight Manors, the gated community that Stéphane and Brian now called home.

"I still can't believe it." Stéphane plucked a white hair from the sleeve of his jacket. "It was a terrible way to go. And such a surprise."

Grahame Cartwright had been their neighbor since the couple moved to Palm Springs. He lived next door, and every morning, Brian and Stéphane had fed him bananas through a glory hole in the fence that separated their two houses. It's a long story. Don't ask!

"A massive heart attack brought on by—" Brian couldn't bring himself to finish the sentence. He felt a lump in his throat. It was too terrible to think about. "I mean, what did Grahame think he was doing?"

"Oh, he knew what he was doing or trying to do. He just never thought it through."

Brian shrugged. "Well, his vanity is what killed him. We all wish we could be young and pretty again, but there are limits. There's a lesson here for all of us to learn from. Cosmetic procedures—if that's what you call them—should only be performed by experts, not carried out in the kitchen by yourself. The sad thing is that Grahame could have used a cream. I'm told that Freshara No 2 comes highly recommended. Only

$46.99 a tube, and you can buy it over the counter. Instead of that, he tried to do it himself on the cheap. You know how much he liked a bargain. I once saw him buy two boxes of tampons—they were Buy One Get One Free. What he did with the tampons is anyone's guess. No, it was his vanity that killed him. Obviously, home-style anal bleaching is not for everyone."

"I don't think he died from bleaching his anus, but by *how* he bleached his anus. There's nothing wrong with wanting your anus to be white and pretty ... as fresh as a daisy. It was the DIY method he used that doomed him."

"You're right. Nothing good comes from parking your bare ass in a bowl of bleach. They say he jumped up so high that the ceiling fan knocked him in the head. That's enough to give anyone a heart attack." Brian struggled with his cuff links. "Damn these things."

"Even after all that, Grahame landed back in the bowl of bleach. His cleaning lady found him three days later. I remember her knocking on our door and screaming. She was in a terrible state."

Stéphane brushed his hair and examined himself in the bathroom mirror. "I remember. She was as white as a ghost. Probably whiter even than Grahame's anus."

"Now, Stéphane, let's see if we can get through this funeral without incident. The last one, your sister, Sr. Bridget, the nun, was a disaster. You made a complete fool of yourself at the graveside, screaming about crucifying mallards. That poor priest was reported and called back to the Vatican over that. He's probably cleaning toilets there now. Either that, or bleaching a cardinal's rectum. Even though it wasn't his fault. It was you who became unhinged and threw a hissy fit."

Stéphane fell silent. He didn't see the point in dragging up the past. Not his past, anyway. Of course, everybody else's past was fair game.

Grahame Cartwright's funeral at St. Theresa's church went off without a hitch. Afterward, his close friends arranged an intimate gathering at Twilight Manors' community hall. Stéphane sipped from a glass of

Chardonnay. "I think this might be Chateau de Urinoir. I detect—yes, a hint of toilet bowl, and—I can't place it. Oh yes, I know, definitely turds. This wine is made from grapes and turds."

Brian ignored him. He was busy talking to a tall skeletal figure in a black suit. "Stéphane! Come and meet Mr. Olson."

Stéphane gently shook Olson's crackling metacarpals. He feared the man's hand might crumble into breadcrumbs. "I'm very pleased to meet you."

Brian smiled. "Mr. Olson is a mortuary beautician. He lives here in Twilight Manors. He made up Grahame for the funeral."

Stéphane's ears perked up. "Oh, that must be an interesting job. Grahame looked quite perky for a corpse. In fact, he looked more alive dead than he ever did alive." Stéphane cringed at his own comment. He had no idea how to properly compliment a mortuary beautician. It's not something they teach you at school. Not in Fort Wayne, Indiana, anyway.

"Thank you." Olson sipped his blood-red Merlot. "I did put a little color into his cheeks. And, of course, I had to do extensive work on the area that was bleached."

Brian was puzzled. "You mean his down-below area?"

"Yes, the bleach did major damage to his genitals and rear end. His testicles were in tatters. He was sat in that bowl of bleach for two days. However, on the bright side, he did succeed in bleaching his anus."

Brian and Stéphane tried not to laugh. Was this a mortician's joke? Olson remained deadpan.

"I'm surprised you touched up his genitals because nobody would see that part of his body. He was wearing a suit in the coffin. Nobody could see his lower regions."

Olson stiffened with pride. "Ah, but I'm a perfectionist. I feel the deceased should always look their best. Aside from his face and genitals, I also re-browned his anus. I used Apricot Nectar lipstick by Maybelline."

Brian looked at his feet. Stéphane stared out the window.

Olson continued. "I don't believe anyone wants to meet their maker with an overly-white anus. What if Grahame turned up at the pearly gates, only to be turned away because of the color of his anus. That may sound like God is being petty but think about it—if God had wanted us to have glistening white anuses, he would have given us glistening white anuses." Olson dabbed his eyes with a handkerchief. "I'm sorry, I get very emotional talking about these things. We are all made in God's image, and if a brown anus is good enough for the Almighty, it should be good enough for the rest of us. Don't get me started on breast implants. I call them the Fun Bags of Satan."

Brian coughed and smiled demurely. "I hear that anal bleaching is very popular with celebrities. Dolly Parton, Jane Fonda, Daniel Radcliffe—"

Stéphane gasped. "—Harry Potter has a bleached anus! I'm shocked."

"Harry Potter's anus is as white as snow." Brian smiled. "If he bent over naked in a blizzard, he'd disappear. Harry Potter has the anus of a snowman. Sean Connery, Billy Connolly, a lot of Scots bleach their anus. Don't know why; it could be a cultural thing. Julia Roberts bleached her anus—Diana Ross—"

The conversation ended there. Exactly where it needed to end.

The following day, the doorbell rang. Stéphane answered it to find a timid, mousy-looking woman in her mid-60s standing on the doorstep. She had a tight perm and wore a duster depicting an array of wildflowers and plump swallows. She wore a pair of frayed blue suede Hush Puppies on her feet. Her pinched face resembled that of a bird. "Hello, I thought I'd better introduce myself. My name is Rosemary. I'm Grahame's sister—Grahame next door. I saw you at the funeral but didn't have time to speak to you. I'm the executor to Grahame's will, and I'll be here for a while selling the house. I didn't want you to think I was an intruder. I will be continuing to work while I'm here. I'm a first-light therapist. I practice music therapy. I worship the sunrise. I help people overcome their fears by singing to them at dawn and drawing down the energy of the three witches who live in the nearby Santa Rosa Mountains."

"Witches?" Brian was rapt. He'd seen *Hocus Pocus.*

"Yes, Witch No 1 is Alessandra, a Brazilian sorceress locked in the mountains by her wicked uncle. She can declutter your future. Witch No 2 is Doofus, the spirit of a metaphysical 19th-century circus clown who can heal the wounds of the past. Doofus is gender non-specific and cradles magic in a multitude of genitals that mirror the testicles of the moon and the vagina of Venus. And Witch No 3 is Trixie, a menstruating virgin who can slap your troubles away with her labia. She will sit on your face and douse you in the mystical blood of womanhood. Did you know my brother well?"

Stephane rallied himself. "Ugh—ugh—Oh yes, we knew Grahame very well. Very sad to lose him like that."

"Yes." Rosemary wiped a tear from her eye. "I'm not entirely surprised he died that way. He was always vain about his appearance. Even as a little boy in Wakonda, South Dakota—population 321—he was the only boy at school who dreamed of being an Avon Lady. 'Ding Dong,' he used to say, 'Can I interest you in buying this eyeshadow?' He rang every doorbell in the town. Of course, he was sent away to Bible camp after that, but whatever they taught him there, it didn't stick. Later, at college, he majored in theater and wrote a play about Doris Day from the viewpoint of one of her dogs. A dachshund named Donut. It was called *Bitch, Bitch, Bitch She's Forgotten to Feed Us Again.*"

"Sounds like a lovely talented boy." Stéphane cleared his throat.

"Never liked sports." Rosemary continued unabated. "Just adored Barbara Streisand—"

Brian interrupted. "—I think we get the picture."

The following morning, Stéphane and Brian sat outside in the garden enjoying breakfast. The bright sun rose over the palm trees, and ravens croaked in the distance. A hummingbird hovered near a feeder. Brian was reflective. "I'm going to miss feeding Grahame bananas through the glory hole."

"Maybe we should block it up. Put a tennis ball in it. It's about the right size. Remember that time we tried feeding him a spoonful of yogurt, and he didn't like it?"

Brian laughed. "He would only eat bananas, wouldn't he? To be honest, we didn't know him very well at all. We only met him face-to-face a couple of times." Brian was interrupted by a woman's voice singing, "Mama Mia." It was coming from next door. "That must be Grahame's sister, Rosemary."

Suddenly there was a slapping sound and a yelp.

"Shh! What was that?" Brian's ears perked up.

Another yelp was followed by three loud slaps.

"What's that noise?" Stephane leapt to his feet and peered through the glory hole. His jaw dropped, and the blood drained from his face. Rosemary kept singing, *"I've been cheated by you since I don't know when. So, I made up my mind, it must come to an end. Look at me now, will I ever learn, I don't know how, but I suddenly lose control. There's a fire within my soul."*

Stéphane beckoned to Brian.

Brian knelt and peered through the glory hole. He clapped his hand over his mouth, then whispered, "Oh my god! She's beating his bare ass with a—what is that?"

Stephane pushed him aside. 'She's beating his ass with an ABBA clog."

"An ABBA clog!" Brian was confused. "What's an ABBA clog? Is that like a blocked sink in Sweden?"

"No, clog—the wooden shoe. Rosemary's beating his bare ass with a wooden ABBA clog. I saw it on Facebook. Someone on the ABBA fan page took a selfie of himself wearing ABBA clogs. Google it if you don't believe me. Their selling ABBA clogs."

Brian shrugged. "I'll never understand Europeans. Who wears wooden shoes?"

"Pinocchio for one."

"Why not wooden socks? Or wooden underwear. Yikes! Splinters."

The man next door yelped again. "Show me some mercy, Mistress Rosemary." The balding man was down on all fours, naked apart from a pair of red stilettos. His rear end was red raw from the beating.

Rosemary, dressed in a leather bustier, fishnet stockings, and teetering on thigh-high boots with spike heels, lifted the ABBA clog again. "No, you've been a very naughty boy. So, I summon up the magic of Witch No 3, Trixie, the menstruating virgin who can slap your troubles away with her labia. Bring her blessings down from the mountains. Let her wrap herself around us and protect us from all harm. Let Trixie fill your sacred bowl with wisdom and heal your withering cells."

"What's she doing now?" Brian was gripped.

Stephane pulled away. "It's complicated. I don't claim to be an expert on heterosexual sadomasochism. Still, my best guess is that he is being slapped around by the labia of a virgin witch."

"Now, there's a sentence you don't hear every day." Brian sniggered. "What kind of therapist is this, Rosemary? When it comes to kinky sex, she beats her brother, hands down. Something terrible must have happened to those two in their childhood. They were probably just a couple of normal *Leave it to Beaver* kids, then one day, while walking along Main Street in some one-horse town, they took a turn into Kinky-Boots Alley, unaware that they were heading down a dark and mysterious path leading to anal bleaching and S&M ABBA clogging. It's mind-boggling."

"I wonder what part of the country they grew up in. What state produces the most sexually adventurous people?"

Brian shrugged. "Vermont? That was a guess."

Rosemary's client started singing. "*Mama Mia, here I go again. My, my, how can I resist you? Mamma mia, does it show again. My, my, just how much I've missed you?*" This was followed by a series of ass-slaps from the ABBA clog.

"That's better." Rosemary's voice was kindly now. "I knew you would sing the song in the end. Good boy. Who wants a reward?"

"I do, Mistress Rosemary."

Brian shoved Stéphane aside and peered through the glory hole. "Oh no!!"

"What's happening?"

"You don't want to know."

"Oh yes, I do; get out the way." Stéphane pushed Brian aside. "Oh my god! She's squatting over his—"

"—Stop! Stop, Stéphane. I don't want to think about it."

"She's peeing on him. I've never seen an old woman peeing before."

Brian smiled weakly. "I guess there's a first time for everything."

Brian and Stéphane returned to the breakfast table. Brian sipped his iced tea. "Let's just pretend that never happened."

"What happened? I never saw a thing. So, what's in the mail today?"

Brian tore open an envelope. "Oh, this sounds interesting. There's an exhibition of Hollywood movie memorabilia at the Palm Springs Art Museum. It's called 'Movie Accessories.' We should go see it. They've got Celia Johnson's hat that she wore in *Brief Encounter*."

"I've memorized every line from that movie. When Laura Jesson returns home on the train, '*I imagined him holding me in his arms. I imagined being with him in all sorts of glamorous circumstances. It was one of those absurd fantasies, just like one has when one is a girl being wooed and married by the idea of one's dreams.*' ... So romantic."

Brian and Stephane swooned.

Next door, Rosemary bellowed an orgasmic scream followed by a short volley of panting gasps. Startled birds took flight. Lizards hid under leaves. Dragonflies trembled over the swimming pool. Two mourning doves flew into each other in a panic and now lay dazed and confused under a palm tree. "'*Mama Mia, here I go again.* Ohh ... Ohh! Ohh!"

Brian buttered a slice of toast. Stéphane pushed his fork into a dish of scrambled eggs.

2

Cactus, My Ass

While Stéphane cleared away the breakfast table, Brian picked an orange from a tree. "Do you think this is ripe yet?"

"I don't know. Try it. What do I know about fruit trees and gardening? Remember our garden in Chicago? For twenty years, I fought that trumpet vine. It spread everywhere. It refused to die. That thing could survive a nuclear war. Cher, cockroaches, Jehovah's Witnesses, and that trumpet vine."

"Yes, I remember you taking an ax to it. I told you to be careful. Limp-wristed men shouldn't be using an ax. I told you that at the time."

"It was a silly accident."

"You were swinging that ax like a crazy man, and it flew out of your hand. You just missed decapitating Choo, next door's Pekingese."

"It was an ugly dog, though. Nobody would have missed it. The dog had a face like a squeezed teabag. And the owner wasn't much better. She looked like Picasso painted her." Stéphane brushed toast crumbs off his T-shirt. "Which reminds me, we need to hire new gardeners. The other ones didn't turn up again this week because of you know what."

"Here we go again. Blaming me. Stéphane, I did not frighten the gardeners away."

"Well, last time they came, you were swimming nude, and that's enough to frighten anyone away."

"I did not frighten the gardeners away. We live in Palm Springs. I'm sure they see lots of naked men in the pools. It's hot here. Bare flesh is the norm."

Stéphane sighed. "Yes, but I'm sure they're not used to seeing that much bare flesh, all in one place, all at one time. They may have thought you were an albino hippopotamus, an endangered species. I can't believe they didn't phone the zoo."

Brian ignored Stéphane, peeled the orange, and bit into it. "It's juicy. I'll pick some, and I'll juice them."

"No, no, no! You're not using my kitchen." Stéphane snapped. "You're banned. I think you caused enough damage when you made a souffle and blew the oven door off. How much did that cost?"

"Ok, I'll pick the oranges, and *you* can juice them."

"That sounds like a much better plan. We can have fresh orange juice for breakfast tomorrow morning." Stéphane disappeared into the kitchen. He was stacking the dishwasher when he heard Brian outside screaming. "Stéphane! Help, help!"

Stéphane ran back into the garden to find Brian hopping around the pool screaming. "What happened? It's a black widow spider, isn't it? Has a black widow spider bitten you? You weren't having sex with it, were you? I read about black widow spiders in *Palm Springs Life*. After copulation, the females sometimes eat their mates—which makes sense when you think about it."

"Stéphane! I have not been bitten by a black widow spider. I tripped and sat on a cactus. Oh, it hurts."

"Brian, you've squashed it. You've killed the cactus."

"I don't care! What about me? You can buy another cactus, but you can't buy another me. Take me to the emergency room. Are cactuses poisonous?"

"How do I know? Do I look like I went to Cactus School? Stop making a big fuss about nothing. It's just ... it's just a little prick in your ass."

"Really, Stéphane, you're now sinking to that level of humor. Really? How old are you? Four! A little prick in my ass ... honey, that's the story of my life. Since I met you, anyway. A little prick in my ass."

Stéphane ignored him. He switched into nurse-mode, or his version of it. "Can you sit down?"

"No! How can I sit down when I've got needles in my ass? I feel like a mad psychotic acupuncturist has kidnapped me. Or some Christian group ... they've kidnapped me to give me aversion therapy to cure my homosexuality."

"Brian, there's no cure for homosexuality. Well, not yours, anyway. It would be easier to find a cure for cancer. If you can't sit down, how can I drive you to the hospital?"

"I want to die!! This is a nightmare. This is worse than the other recurring nightmare I had. The one where I get chased through the streets of Baltimore by topless women carrying cabbages."

"I'll let that go without comment. Look, I'll pull the car out into the street, then you'll have more space to maneuver yourself into it. Maybe you can curl up across the back seat. Or ... I've got it! I'll attach the roof rack. Maybe you could lie on top of the car."

"You're not strapping me to the roof rack. I'm not a canoe, Stéphane. Do I look like a canoe?"

"A little bit. The more I think about it, the more you look like a coal barge."

"Just get me to the emergency room."

Stéphane backed the car out of the garage and into the street. Brian attempted to curl up in the back. "I can't do it. The car is too small. We need a bigger car."

"Don't blame the car, Brian. You can't get in because you're too fat."

"I'm not fat. I'm a Bear."

Stéphane rolled his eyes. "Brian, you can see your ass from space. The Russians have a nuclear missile aimed at your ass. It's target number four after the United States Capitol building, the White House, the Pentagon, then it's Brian's ass. The Statue of Liberty has a smaller ass than you. Your ass is big enough to have its own zip code and mayor."

Alice Springer, her wife, Jennie Fisher, and Mitzi, their demented chihuahua, turned the corner onto the street. "Stéphane!" Alice called out to him. "What a beautiful morning. Another day in paradise."

"It is."

Brian was still struggling, trying to climb into the car's back seat.

"What's happening with Brian?"

"He sat on a cactus. I'm trying to get him to the emergency room, but I don't know how to get him there. He can't sit down."

"Cactus needles can be very painful." Jennie sighed. "They're such angry plants. If cactuses were human, you might say they were grumpy. But, Brian, if you ever again feel the need to sit on a plant, then may I suggest snapdragons."

"Or pansies." Alice smiled. "Snapdragons or pansies. They're squidgy. Either of those won't send you to the emergency room."

"You make it sound like I sat on the cactus on purpose. That I got up this morning and thought, 'What plant am I going to sit on today?' Oh, I'll sit on this spiky one. That'll work." Brian wanted to crawl into a hole and die.

A man appeared, turning the corner at the end of the street. He was speed-walking. "Good morning, my name's Garth Barker. Is there anything I can help you with? I fought in Vietnam, so I'm used to solving problems. You might say I'm a problem solver. Give me a problem, and I'll solve it. I remember this one time there was a leaky faucet in a brothel in Da Nang. I was in the middle of humping a delightful whore named Hong, which means pink rose in English, when I heard a dripping faucet. Solved that dripping faucet problem, married Hong, and the rest is history. Then there was this other whore—different brothel—while I was humping her, I noticed a leak in the ceiling. The drip, drip, drip was putting me off my stride. I always carried a bag of tools with me back then—anyway, I climbed off her and dealt with the leak. Then I jumped back on and finished. But the best time was when I was humping a whore in Saigon. The brothels there were dilapidated, which is where I shone with my problem-solving. I was humping this whore, and suddenly, the whole shack started leaning over. I managed to save the day with that one, too. I've just moved into Puesta De Sol with my wife, Hong—I believe everyone calls it Twilight Manors. I'm delighted to meet my new neighbors. So, is there a problem here? You're all looking a little lost."

Jaws dropped.

Stéphane smiled nervously. "Well, yes, my husband sat on a cactus. We need to get him to the emergency room. The problem is that he can't sit down. So he can't get in the car."

Ted laughed. "Husband, hey! Good for you. We had a couple of nelly boys in our platoon. I've sampled some of that myself, in a brothel in Hanoi. I was humping this young guy one time when I noticed his door was squeaking. So I sorted that problem out. Why? Because I'm a problem solver. Now, what are we going to do with your husband and his cactus impregnated ass? Have you thought about strapping him to a roof rack like a canoe?"

George Montgomery, their next-door neighbor, was checking his mailbox. He saw Stéphane trying to shove Brian into the car. "Can I help?"

"Brian has sat on a cactus and needs to go to the emergency room, but he can't sit down in the car or lie down curled up in the back seat because he's too fat."

"Stéphane, I keep telling you I'm not fat. I'm a Bear."

"Keep telling yourself that. When you turn up in London's Paddington Station with an old hat, a battered suitcase, and wearing a duffel coat, then you're a bear. When you start raiding picnic tables in Yellowstone National Park, then you're a bear. An inability to walk past a Krispy Kreme store without going in does not make you a bear. It makes you a pig."

"That's it! Go on, make fun of my weight like they all did back in school. Fat Brian, that's what they called me. You're just as much a bully as those kids at my school. You should be ashamed of yourself. What would you say if I called you a skinny little nelly boy?"

"What would I say? I'd say thank you very much for noticing, and can you recommend a good manicurist. I've just chipped a nail."

George thought for a moment. "Have you thought about strapping him to a roof rack like a canoe?"

Brian tugged at his hair. "How many times do I have to say this? I am not a canoe."

"I know! I've got it! Wait a minute." George disappeared around the side of his house and returned with a woman. She was built like a brick shithouse. "This is Margarita. She was a stunt-double for Jason Momoa in *Game of Thrones*. She's also my gardener. She said she'll drive you to the hospital."

"Isabella!" Margarita hollered.

Another woman appeared from George's back garden. She was petite, pretty, and had long black hair tied in a ponytail hanging almost down to her waist. "What do you want?"

"I'm taking this guy to the emergency room. He sat on a cactus. I'll be back in half an hour. Cut that ficus back."

Garth and Margarita hoisted Brian into the back of her truck. He lay flat on his stomach amongst the garden tools and severed tree limbs. Ten minutes later, the truck pulled up outside the emergency room at Desert Regional Hospital. Margarita pulled on Brian's feet, dragging him across the back of the truck until he fell and was standing up. Brian felt like a sack of potatoes.

Stéphane arrived in his car seconds later. "Thank you so much. It was very kind of you to do this. I've just had a thought. We need to hire new gardeners—once a week—would you be interested?"

"Of course, we'll start Monday morning. Gracias."

Margarita climbed into her truck and drove away, leaving Stéphane and Brian standing outside the emergency room.

"Stéphane, what were you talking to that woman about?"

"She's our new gardener. We now have lesbiana gardeners. They're coming on Mondays, so no more nude swimming on Mondays. You don't want to frighten the lesbians. They might *react*. I can't think of anything more degrading than being kicked in the nuts by Jason Momoa's stunt double."

3

I Scream for Ice Cream

The following morning, Brian perched on a cushion at the breakfast table. All the cactus needles had been removed from his buttocks, but he was still tender. "I can't believe they put Elmer's glue on my ass."

"That's how they remove the cactus needles. With glue. It could have been worse. There were people in the emergency room with far more serious problems than you. What about that woman who fell off the ladder and landed on the George Forman grill—third-degree burns? It was awful. Ugly shoes she was wearing too. White pumps and that black bow." Stéphane screwed up his face. "Some people just don't think before leaving the house. Did she even consider that other people would have to look at those shoes? I almost brought up my breakfast. And who designed them in the first place? It wasn't Manolo Blahnik. I can tell you that. Or Luis Onofre."

"And why was she climbing a ladder in white pumps anyway?"

"Brian, some people are clueless. She would never have fallen off the ladder and landed on the George Forman Grill if she'd been wearing nice shoes. Now she's got a face like a deep-dish pizza. Good luck finding shoes to go with that face."

Brian changed the subject. "What did you think of Mr. Olson, the mortuary beautician at Grahame's funeral?"

"Does he have a first name? Boris, Gloomlops, maybe?"

"He must have, but I have no idea what it is. He introduced himself to me as Mr. Olson."

"Well, he certainly looks like a mortuary beautician. Lurch from *The Addams Family*. Some people look like their jobs, don't they? I can spot a librarian from a block away. Bookish, glasses—"

"Oh, Stéphane, that's a stereotype. But you're right about Mr. Olson. He does look like a mortuary beautician. Creepy, wiry, and brittle. It got me thinking about how I'm getting you made up after you die."

"Who said I'm going first?"

"It's always the skinny one who goes first. Maybe Mr. Olson can make you up as a circus clown. Or Tammy Faye. How would you get Mr. Olson to make me up?"

"Oh, that's easy, Bette Davis as Baby Jane Hudson in *Whatever Happened to Baby Jane?*" Stéphane was interrupted by Rosemary singing in the garden next door.

"'*Can you hear the drums, Fernando? I remember long ago another starry night like this. In the firelight, Fernando.*'"

THWACK! ... Yelp!

Stéphane ran to the glory hole. "Brian, Rosemary has another client for her 'musical therapy.'" Through the hole, he saw a man down on all fours being beaten with the ABBA clog. He wore nothing but a dog collar and a horse's saddle strapped to his back.

Rosemary continued. "'*You were humming to yourself and softly strumming your guitar. I could hear the distant drums. And sounds of bugle calls were coming from afar.*'"

THWACK! ... Yelp!

"Now tell Mistress Rosemary again how your momma took your toys away and threw them in the trash. Just because you wet the bed. Tell Mistress Rosemary about that. Take yourself back to that little boy you once were. Coming home from school and finding your mother throwing all your toys away. Now tell your momma what you should have told her back then."

The man's voice cracked with emotion. "Momma, please don't throw away my toys. I promise I'll never wet the bed again."

Rosemary lifted the ABBA clog. "No, no, no!"

THWACK! ... Yelp!

"Tell your momma what you really wanted to say to her."

"Momma, you're a heartless bitch."

"That's more like it. Tell momma what you really think."

"Give me my toys back, you stupid fucked-up drug-addicted hooker."

"That's it, you tell her! Tell her!"

"You touch my toys again, and I'll slap the shit out of you!" The man broke down in tears.

"Good boy! Let it all out. Emote! Emote! Now, sing along with me. Let's sing the bad times away. *'Can you hear the drums, Fernando? I remember long ago another starry night like this. In the firelight, Fernando.'*"

Back at the breakfast table, Brian poured cornflakes into a bowl. "Is it the same guy?"

"No, this is a different client altogether. This one has a birthmark on his ass, shaped like Texas."

"Same thing with the ABBA clog, though."

"Yes. I'm glad we didn't block up the glory hole. The neighbors are better than anything on TV." Stéphane sliced open an envelope and read the glossy card. "This came in the mail yesterday."

"What is it?"

"It's about the exhibition of Hollywood memorabilia at Palm Springs Art Museum. They've got Celia Johnson's hat from *Brief Encounter*. They've also got Peter Fonda's legendary Harley Chopper from *Easy Rider*. We should go."

"Let's go tomorrow. It'll take my mind off cactuses. Today, we go for ice cream."

Ice Cream was a weekly ritual in the Stéphane and Brian household.

Stéphane parked the car on the tourist strip on Palm Canyon Drive. Palm Springs residents mostly avoid this strip as it's crowded with families hellbent on having a good time. Most visitors don't experience temperatures of 120 degrees at home, so the desert sun has a strange effect on them. It overheats their brains, turns them into ticking time bombs, and causes them to buy things for their kids just to shut them up. Tourists are easy to spot from their ensemble choices; their outfits are a hodge-podge of colors and styles that shouldn't be in the same room together, let alone on the same body. And socks and sandals. Lots of socks and lots of sandals. On this strip of Palm Canyon Drive, you can buy a "But it's a dry heat" T-shirt, have your tarot read, dine on mediocre, overpriced food, or drink yourself into a stupor at the straight bars where local bands play "Jolene," "Tragedy," and "The Final Countdown."

The Cold Comfort Shake Rattle and Roll Ice Cream Parlor is the best in the Coachella Valley. Brian liked the Almond Joy shake and Stéphane, the Key Lime Pistachio cone.

Stéphane pushed open the door. The parlor was crowded. It usually was. When they eventually reached the counter, they ordered and sat at a seat in the window. It overlooked the sidewalk with its buzzing swarm of frantic tourists. A young woman with blue hair and a pierced nose delivered their cold concoctions.

Stéphane licked his ice cream cone. "Did you see that guy serving behind the counter?"

"The blond with the dragon tattoo on his arm?"

"Yes, that's him."

"What about him? He's new. I haven't seen him before."

"He looks like one of my second cousins back in Fort Wayne, Indiana. He was knee-high to a grasshopper last time I saw him."

"It's not him, though."

"Oh no, he just looks like him."

"Whoever he is, he's almost as delicious as this shake. Next time, I might order a banana split with a cherry on top."

"Brian, you lost your cherry decades ago. Somewhere around the time that JFK was assassinated, wasn't it? The Cold War was going on. The year *Move Over, Darling* came out. Before microwaves."

Sitting in the window, Brian and Stéphane people-watched and played their favorite game, Politically Incorrect; basically, the two act as fashion police and critique passers-by. Stéphane pointed. "Look at him. What does he think he's doing wearing that outfit? He's an eyesore. Who comes out in broad daylight wearing a baseball cap, a buttoned-down shirt, a cardigan—yes, a cardigan in Palm Springs—shorts, and tassel loafers?"

"Tassel loafers are a hanging offense."

Stéphane palmed his face. "And look at the wife. Safe to say that she won't be winning any beauty contests. She looks like she was dragged through a hedge backward. Do they have hairbrushes where she lives? Or irons. It looks like her dress was made by four color-blind bricklayers who hate each other."

Brian giggled. He loved playing Politically Incorrect. "And look at the kids! Butt ugly little Oompa Loompas. I bet they're a petri dish of disease. Kids usually are. Oh, I'd better shut up. They're coming in here."

The tourist family entered the Cold Comfort Shake Rattle and Roll Ice Cream Parlor and stood at the counter. The father took charge. "What do you want, Martha Mae?"

The little girl picked her nose. "I want chocolate with everything."

"And what about you, Jimmy James?"

"Peanut butter." He clapped his hands.

The mother asked for two scoops of Rocky Road.

Brian nudged Stéphane. "Look, look, look, the mother."

The woman's dress was wedged in between her buttocks.

"Her ass is chewing her dress." Stéphane giggled. "Maybe we're all going to get sucked in. Maybe that's how the world ends. The End Times.

The Great Beast—666. We all thought the world would end with a nuclear war, plague or the zombie apocalypse. But maybe the world ends when it's sucked into the ass of a tourist. Oh, the horror of it all. I can see the movie now, *The Tourist Who Inhaled.*"

Brian laughed. "There are worse things than being sucked into the ass of a tourist."

Brian and Stéphane giggled like four-year-olds.

The family sat down at a table near Stéphane and Brian. When their ice creams arrived, Martha Mae was so excited that she jumped up and down and tripped. Her waffle cone flew through the air and landed splat-side-down in Brian's lap. Brian jumped up, and the waffle cone slid onto his stool. Then he lost his balance and sat down on the waffle cone.

Stéphane laughed. "Brian, it looks like you had an accident. Like you never quite made it to the bathroom. We'll stop on the way home and buy you some diapers. Depend. If their good enough for June Allyson's little dribbles, they're good enough for you."

The smile drained from Stéphane's face when Jimmy James, upset by his sister falling, threw his ice cream cone at Stéphane. It landed on his head, then slid down his neck, his shirt, and landed on his butt, leaving a peanut butter brown stain.

A woman, sat next to them in the window, leaned across. "I've been listening to you two talking, and that—" She pointed to the stains on the men's pants. "That is called karma, boys. That's instant karma. John Lennon wrote a song about it."

Brian wiped himself down with a napkin but only made it worse. "How will we get back to the car with ice cream stains all over us? What will the tourists think?"

"They'll think we've pooped ourselves. All we can do is walk as quickly as possible, eyes straight ahead—nothing to see here. Behave like it's normal. 'Oh darling, everyone's wearing their own poop these days.' Think of it as a fashion accessory, like a brooch. A shitty brooch. Talking of shitty brooches, look at that woman over there." Stéphane pointed out the window.

"Oh my God, that's ugly. What is it? A silver dragon brooch on that boring dress! I say dress, but it's a schmata, really. Something you'd wear to clean the stove."

As they weaved their way through swarms of tourists, many of them stared at Brian and Stéphane's stained pants. A husband and his wife sniggered. A little girl ran along beside them. She pointed at Brian. "Look, Mommy, that man's gone poopsie in his pants."

Brian froze. He was bullied mercilessly at school. Those days were over. He decided many years ago that he would never allow himself to be bullied again. Not even by an evil little monster with pigtails and a Hello Kitty purse. "Look here, Missie! You're probably wondering why we have brown stains on the seat of our pants. Do I tell her, Stéphane, or do you want to do it?"

"You do it."

Brian turned back to the little girl. "Let me tell you this. It's not ice cream. We have brown stains on our pants because we've both pooped ourselves. We're old men, and we're proud of the fact that we poop ourselves. Aren't we, Stephane?"

"Yes, very proud. When we want to poop, we just poop, wherever we are. We pooped in a bakery the other day, didn't we, Brian? We were buying Danish pastries, and next thing you know, there's poop running down my leg."

"I remember that. The French bakery where they make the footschlong chocolate eclairs. Mmm! Delicious."

"Brian, you mean footlong chocolate éclair, not footschlong chocolate éclair."

"Sorry, Stéphane, I was thinking of something else. I'm wearing my Freudian slippers."

The parents covered the little girl's ears and hustled her away along the sidewalk. The mother turned. "You should be ashamed of yourselves. Talking like that in front of a child."

"No, she should be ashamed of herself for shit-shaming us. What do you think, Stéphane?"

"I agree. You should sit your daughter down and explain to her that making fun of old people who shit themselves is unacceptable."

Brian waved. "Bye, Felicia! Stephane, they're running away from us. Do you think it was something we said?"

4
"Movie Accessories"

The following day, Stéphane and Brian parked the car in downtown Palm Springs. They walked two blocks to the Palm Springs Art Museum. A large banner hung outside. It read, "Movie Accessories." As they approached the entrance, a young man pushed Brian aside and ran off down the street. "What was that about? He was in a hurry."

"Did you see who that was? That's the guy serving in the ice cream parlor yesterday. The one who looks like my second cousin in Fort Wayne. The cute one."

"No, that's not him. The guy in the ice cream parlor was clean-shaven. That guy had a goatee."

"But didn't it look fake? The guy had blond hair, piercing blue eyes, and a black goatee. Who has blond hair and a black goatee, or was it dark brown?"

Brian agreed. "It did look fake. Now I come to think about it, it was hanging off his face."

"He was holding the goatee on. He kept pressing it with his fingers. As if it was going to fall off. It was definitely the guy working in the ice cream parlor. I recognize the tattoo. What happened to good manners? I'll tell you what happened. Good manners died out when the Internet started." Stéphane homed in on one of his favorite topics. "We've lost the ability to communicate with each other. Now we're being forced to accept new concepts like 'virtual' and 'digital.' Things that go against our natural instincts. We're social animals, not robots."

A young man, staring at his phone, pushed Stéphane aside. "Get out of the way!"

Stéphane smiled and stuck out his foot. The young man tripped, stumbled, and fell flat on his face. Blood gushed from his nose. "Oh, I'm sorry young man." Then Stéphane "accidentally" stepped on the young man's phone. "Oh dear, I'm such a clumsy old man." Stéphane stomped on the phone again. "See, I'm so old and forgetful that I stood on your phone twice." He stomped on the phone again. "I keep doing it. It must be because I'm old and stupid. I'm repeating myself. I should be put in a home with all the other old people who are worthless and teetering on the precipice of death."

The young man jumped to his feet, picked up what was left of his phone, then ran away with blood streaming from his nose. "You old twot."

Stéphane rallied. "Yes, young man, I may be a twot, but at least my phone works. Unfortunately, yours seems to be broken." Stéphane waved his phone. "Now, where was I before I was so rudely interrupted."

Stéphane was again pushed aside, this time by a girl texting. Again, Stéphane stuck out his foot. The teenage girl splatted onto the path. Blood everywhere. A woman tried to help her up. "Maybe you should look where you're going instead of looking at your damn phone. They should do something about this pathway here. It's dangerous."

Stéphane was then bumped a third time. Yet another young man went down. He fell on top of the teenage girl and broke his glasses. Stéphane "accidentally" stepped on his phone as well. "Oh, I'm so sorry, I'm such a clumsy old man. I apologize for taking up space in *your* world."

Brian stepped in. "I know you're having fun with this, but—"

"—Brian, I could do this all day."

"I know you could."

"I'm actually getting a boner. I think I've discovered a new fetish— tripping up annoying young people." Stéphane squeezed his crotch.

"Yep, I'm getting a stiffy. This is the most fun I've had since we played miniature golf with that one-legged beekeeper we met in Disney World. Remember him? And the problem with the ball getting stuck in the little windmill."

"How could I possibly forget. I remember it as if it was only yesterday. I remember the ambulance coming, the fire brigade trying to get the beekeeper's artificial leg out of the windmill."

"Well, it wasn't my fault that he got frustrated, kicked it, and got his leg stuck. That was all on him."

"And then his glass eye fell out, and you putted it into the hole."

"It was fun, though, wasn't it?"

"Not for him, it wasn't."

Inside the museum, Brian and Stéphane entered the first room. A banner hanging from the ceiling read FOOTWEAR. Among the exhibits was Tom Hanks's red shoe from the movie *The Man with One Red Shoe*; James Dean's boots from *Rebel Without a Cause*; and the white lace-up Edwardian-style boots worn by Julie Andrews in *Mary Poppins*. But the prize was the two-meter-tall stiletto from *The Adventures of Priscilla Queen of the Desert*. A group of gay men gathered around the shoe, then one of them burst into song, "*Hey lady, you lady. Cursing at your life. You're a discontented mother. And a regimented wife*" ... while he juggled three ping pong balls.

It was very much a Palm Springs moment.

Under a banner reading HEADWEAR, they saw Celia Johnson's hat from *Brief Encounter*; Oddjob's bowler in *Goldfinger*; Basil Rathbone's deerstalker from *The Adventures of Sherlock Holmes*; Tony Curtis's hat in *Some Like it Hot*, and Harrison Ford's fedora in *Indiana Jones and the Temple of Doom*. When Stéphane saw Audrey Hepburn's hat from *My Fair Lady*, he clutched his pearls and gasped. "Look, Brian, I can hardly breathe. It's fabulous."

"That would really suit me."

"No, no, no, you couldn't get away with wearing that hat. It takes poise, panache, and style to do it justice—three things you lack, Brian. If you don't mind me saying so."

"Actually, I do mind you saying so. I'd look amazing in that hat. I could wear that hat on the runway at the Oscars or when I go grocery shopping. It suits any occasion."

"You'd look like a balloon with a pancake balanced on top of it."

Brian dropped the subject. There was no winning when Stéphane was in this mood.

The next room had an overhead banner reading ADULT ACCESSORIES. NOT SUITABLE FOR SOME AUDIENCES. A security guard checked IDs.

Brian was confused. "Stéphane, what does that mean? Adult accessories."

"I just overheard someone say that these exhibits were not in movies but were items that stars left in their dressing rooms or trailers after filming was over. Intimate items. Things you keep in a box under the bed. This is the personal collection of one of the backstage crew. He's in his 90s now. He secretly collected these over the years."

Brian and Stéphane showed their IDs to the security guard and pulled back the curtain. Inside, Stéphane gasped. "Oh my god, what is that?"

Brian read the label on the first exhibit. "This was found in John Wayne's trailer when he made *True Grit*. It's a dildo. Was John Wayne gay?"

"I hope not. He was a right-winger. But talking of gay, look at this! Rock Hudson's crotchless panties. Who knew?"

"No surprises there. Oh, look at that!" Stéphane pointed to an exhibit in a shadow box. "It's Annette Funicello's nipple clamps. They found these after she made *Beach Blanket Bingo* with Frankie Avalon."

"A Mouseketeer with hardwired nipples! Whatever next? Frankie Avalon was such a dish."

"Brian, you're like a cat with a dish full of cream."

"Frankie Avalon was a dish full of cream—this is the best exhibition ever! Any other Disney memorabilia here? Snow White's butt plug—Tinkerbell's anal beads?"

Just then, the alarms sounded. Everybody froze. Seconds later, security guards locked down the entrances and exits to the museum. The police arrived and herded everyone into the lobby. A cop stepped forward. "Can I get everyone's attention, please? Don't move, everyone stay exactly where you are. This is a lockdown. I'm sorry to inconvenience you all, but one of the exhibits has gone missing."

A woman asked. "What is it that's missing?"

"I'm sorry, that's all the information we have at the moment."

An hour later, Brian and Stéphane were released after being voluntarily searched. The "Movie Accessories" exhibit was temporarily closed.

5

A Floater in the Pool

The following day at the breakfast table, Stephane picked up the *Desert Sun*. A headline on the front page read, 'Donna Reed's Pubic Wig Snatched.'

Stephane lowered the paper. "Have you seen this? Remember what happened at the art museum yesterday? The lockdown. This is what it was all about—someone stole Donna Reed's pubic wig from the 'Movie Accessories' exhibition."

"Pubic wig! Donna Reed wore a merkin, a public wig!! What?"

Stéphane read the article. "Apparently, there was a celebrity craze for them in the 1960s. It started in England with Diana Rigg, Julie Andrews, and Honor Blackman."

"Didn't Honor Blackman play Pussy Galore in *Goldfinger*?"

"That's her. I wonder if she was wearing the pubic wig when she played her *Goldfinger* Pussy?"

Brian shrugged. "Well, that's the question on everyone's lips this morning after reading that article. I never knew such a thing existed. I wonder if Hollywood male stars wore them. I can see Gregory Peck wearing a pubic wig in *Moby Dick*."

"*Moby Dick* was before the pubic wig fad."

"You don't know, Gregory Peck could have been a pioneer. I can also see Richard Burton and Elizabeth Taylor in *Taming of the Shrew* wearing matching pubic wigs. So did they find Donna Reed's wig?"

"It says here in the paper that the wig had a tracking device on it, which they found out in the Mojave desert. But no wig. It's still missing."

Brian laughed. "Who would steal a thing like that? I mean, it can't be worth much. I suppose its value is that it was worn by Donna Reed."

"Some people will steal anything that's not nailed down. Remember in Chicago when we left that cake out in the rain."

Brian smiled. "The one with the sweet, green icing flowing down—"

"—That's the one. That got stolen."

"It wasn't stolen. It melted."

Next door, Rosemary started her first-light therapy session. "*Ooh. You can dance. You can jive. Having the time of your life. Ooh, see that girl. Watch that scene. Digging the dancing queen.*"

THWACK ... Yelp.

After a couple of verses, Rosemary stopped singing. There was a long ominous silence, lasting a minute or so. Then a splashing sound. Brian dangled a slice of toast from his fingertips. "I think she's jumped into the pool."

A few moments later, Rosemary screamed. Stéphane ran to the glory hole and peered through it. He could see Rosemary by the pool with her face in her hands. "Oh no! What am I going to do? Help! Help!"

Stéphane and Brian ran out into the street, through the side gate, and into the garden next door. They found Rosemary wringing her hands and her "patient" floating face-down in the pool. "I answered the phone. It was the realtor. Someone wants to see the house. When I got back, I found him in the pool. I left him here by this chair. I told him to stay still and not be a naughty boy. He must have wriggled over and fallen in."

Brian waded out into the pool. "No pulse. He's gone. Stéphane call the police and an ambulance. It might be an idea to drag him out of the pool and remove the chastity belt, the ball gag, the handcuffs, and the diaper."

"No, Brian, we can't touch anything. I know what I'm talking about. I watch *Law and Order*. I'm channeling Olivia Benson. I've got her cheekbones."

Brian climbed out of the pool. "I'm drenched. I'm going next door to dry off and change."

"Is everything alright back there?" Alice Springer was standing at the gate. "We were out walking Mitzi and heard somebody screaming. Brian, what happened? You're soaking wet."

"Ask Stéphane. I'll be back. I'm going next door to dry off and change my clothes. There's been an accident. Someone's fallen in the pool and drowned."

Stéphane comforted Rosemary. "Don't worry, this will all get sorted out. The police see things like this all the time, especially in Palm Springs. Freak S&M accidents are a dime a dozen here."

Alice Springer, her wife, Jennie, and Mitzi, their annoying long-haired, one-eyed chihuahua, joined them by the pool. They tried desperately to ignore the fact that Rosemary was wearing a leather bustier and carrying an ABBA clog. Jennie zoned out. Alice averted her eyes and focused on the body in the pool. "My goodness, what happened here?"

Stéphane dialed 911.

Alice screwed up her eyes. "Jennie, is he wearing a diaper?"

Jennie looked. "Yes, it looks like it. It's slipped down to his knees."

"It's probably IBS, Irritable Bowel Syndrome. Some people are so afflicted with it that they have to wear a diaper. In fact, Mitzi had to wear a diaper for a while, didn't she, Jennie?"

"Yes. Sore tummy. But it kept falling off. They don't make chihuahua-sized diapers. So we had to use thong liner maxi pads."

"With string and safety pins. It was more of a contraption than a diaper. It's amazing that they can land a man on the moon, but they can't design diapers for small mammals. What if your hamster gets a leaky butt?"

When Brian returned, he glared at Mitzi. Mitzi glared at Brian. They hated each other. They had a history. It was as if something terrible had occurred between them in a previous life. Now, in this life, they were both hellbent on revenge. Mitzi saw Brian and barked. Then she freed herself from her leash and headed for Brian's ankle. Brian stepped aside at the last moment, and Mitzi ran into the pool.

"Mitzi! Oh, Mitzi!" Alice was frantic. "Brian, save Mitzi. Jump in."

"I'm not going anywhere near that dog. She hates me." Brian smiled as Mitzi floundered. This could be the end of his nemesis. Mitzi's comeuppance. Good riddance. The dog swam in circles, then turned toward the drowned man, struggled onto his back, then laid there panting. She looked like a canine pirate stranded on Dead Man's Island.

"Look, Mitzi's been saved." Jennie clapped her hands.

"Hello! Can I help? Is there a problem here?" It was Garth Barker, the Vietnam war veteran, and problem solver. "I was out walking, and I heard a ruckus."

"Yes." Alice took a deep breath. "Mitzi has fallen into the pool."

Garth looked at the pool. "Umm ... is that Mitzi sitting on the back of a floater?"

"Yes, I know it's an odd thing to say, but the dead man saved her. If he hadn't been dead, Mitzi would have drowned."

"Who's the dead man?" Garth walked around the pool. "Has anyone checked that he's dead? I've read about cases where someone has gone into a deep sleep, everyone thought they were dead, and they were buried alive."

Stéphane sighed. "Is it possible to fall asleep underwater?"

Garth pointed. "Is he wearing a diaper?"

Rosemary had visibly calmed down. Though, she was still trembling. "It was an accident. We were having a therapy session. I left him here and answered the phone."

Stéphane cleared his throat. "Just tell the police it was an accident. Say you answered the phone, and when you came back, you found him floating in the pool. Just tell them the truth. That you were slapping him around with an ABBA clog and singing *Dancing Queen*. I'm sure they'll believe you."

Garth scratched his head. "So where does the diaper come in? Is that handcuffs? Oh, wait a minute, I know what this is. I get it. I saw this in a brothel in Saigon. I was humping this whore when I noticed her ceiling fan wasn't working. So being a problem solver, I repaired that. I also noticed a man walking around the brothel wearing a diaper. It's called autonepiophilia—men who get a kick out of wearing a diaper. Toilet love. For them, filling a diaper is just another way of saying 'I love you.'"

Alice looked puzzled. "I've heard of this, but I find it interesting that it's always men, isn't it? You never hear of women wearing diapers and dying in pools. Why is that? Oh, look, Mitzi has fallen asleep on the dead man's back. She looks so peaceful there. Jennie, take a picture."

Brian interrupted. "Mitzi seems to have calmed down. The dead man has the big sleep and Mitzi is having a prolonged nap. I'd rather it was the other way around, but here we are?"

"Mitzi, come to mommy." Jennie beckoned from the edge of the pool. "Come to mommy."

An ambulance arrived. Two wide-eyed medics approached the pool; one, a woman in her mid-thirties with her hair tightly pulled back into a bun. The other, a man barely out of his teens with flaming red hair and flashing emerald-green eyes.

"What happened here?" The young woman stifled a laugh.

"There's been an accident. He drowned." Stéphane also tried to keep a straight face.

The second medic grinned. "Why does the dead man have a dog sleeping on his back?

Alice pointed. "That's Mitzi. She climbed onto the man's back after he died. Of course, she had nothing to do with his death. I mean, she didn't push him into the pool or anything."

The male medic stripped down to his boxer shorts and waded out into the water. But when he got close to the body, Mitzi woke up and barked and growled at him. "Why are you getting so angry with me. Let me pick you up." Mitzi bit the medic's finger.

The police arrived, a silver daddy with a 1970s porn mustache and a younger one who looked like Antonio Banderas—he had the right amount of everything in exactly the right place.

Brian and Stéphane swooned. Brian fanned himself. "Are they real cops, or did you order me a pair of strippers?"

"Real cops."

"Looking at those two, I'm getting the urge to be burgled, if you know what I mean. I can see them entering my back door with their weapons cocked."

"I know exactly what you mean."

Brian swooned. "Oh, but the young redhead medic with the green eyes—I could dive deep into those eyes and swim around."

"Oh Brian, the last thing that young man needs is some fat old trout like you swimming around in his eyes. He needs someone with a girly figure, like *moi*."

The redhead in the pool grew increasingly frustrated. Every time he approached Mitzi, she snapped at him with her razor-sharp needle teeth. Finally, frustrated, he climbed out. "We can't get the body out of the water until someone does something about this dog. Maybe we should tase it."

"No!" Alice cried out, but it was too late. The silver daddy cop tased Mitzi. She shot through the air like a pebble from a slingshot. She landed on top of a ten-foot-high palm tree scaring off a raven who was roosting there.

Brian smiled to himself. Fingers crossed—Mitzi was dead.

Margarita, the new gardener, shouted over the fence from next door. "Stéphane, just letting you know that we're making a start on your garden. I recognize your voice."

Stéphane called back. "There's been an accident here. Someone has drowned in the pool. And there's a chihuahua stuck in a palm tree. She's been tased—long story. Do you have a ladder?"

"Of course, hold on, we're coming around."

Margarita, and her partner, Isabella, joined the others around Rosemary's pool. Margarita carried a ten-foot ladder.

Stéphane pointed to a palm tree. "She's up there. She may be fried. Or at the very least, in a confused state of mind."

Garth stepped forward. "Do you want me to climb up and get her? I'm a problem solver. This won't be the first time I've saved a creature in distress. I was once in this brothel in Ha Long. I was humping this whore every which way when I noticed her goldfish was floating in the bowl. I climbed off her and gave the goldfish the kiss of life. Giving the kiss of life to a goldfish is a bit like eating pussy. You use the same facial muscles. I even gave the goldfish a bit of tongue. After I saved the poor goldfish, I climbed back on the whore and rode her all the way to Cum City."

A shocked silence fell over the gathered throng.

Margarita regained her composure. "No, we can manage, thank you. Isabella, see if you can get the dog down."

Isabella climbed the ladder, picked up Mitzi by her back legs, and shook her. "I think it's dead."

Alice fainted and fell into the pool. Jennie reached out to grab her, then lost her balance. She also fell into the pool.

Brian buried his face in his hands. "Now we've got a corpse and two old lesbians in the pool. Can this get any worse? All we need now is Cirque du Soleil and the Mormon Tabernacle Choir to fall in. That's when the party really begins."

The medics and police helped the two women out of the pool.

Isabella shook Mitzi again. "No, wait a minute, it's breathing. And it's angry. Can somebody take this thing off me? Quickly, before I throw it back into the pool."

Brian's heart sank. The dog was still breathing. Even 50,000 volts couldn't kill Mitzi. Brian had already chosen an outfit for Mitzi's funeral. "That animal could survive a tank rolling over it."

A soaking wet Alice petted Mitzi. "She seems alright. Her tongue's hanging out of her mouth, and she's dribbling, so that's a good sign, isn't it? Poor Mitzi."

The truth was that Mitzi was plotting her revenge against Brian. And the payback would be lethal, swift, and would come without warning. Nothing can stop a one-eyed chihuahua with a grudge.

The medics removed the body from the pool and zipped it up into a body bag.

The silver-haired daddy cop took Rosemary aside. After a brief conversation, he turned to the young cop. "It looks like a freak S&M accident. Remember that woman in Rancho Mirage who nailed her husband's foreskin to a toilet seat? That was consensual. It's the same thing here. Just a bit of fun gone wrong."

"I think that's for the courts to decide. Does the deceased have a name?"

The older cop rifled through the dead man's clothes and found his wallet. "His name is Allan Hollybush, and there's a blood transfusion refusal card. He's a Jehovah's Witness. An elder. There's a photograph. It looks like he was married with three kids."

"Typical hypocrites." Stéphane threw up his hands. "So where in the Bible does it say its ok to get your diapered ass beaten with an ABBA clog?"

"It's in Ecclesetesticles. '*And God said go forth my dancing queen into Fernando's dungeon where you will be smitten by an ABBA clog ... you naughty boy.*'" Brian smiled.

Brian and Stephane never saw Rosemary again. The following day the FOR SALE sign was taken down by the realtor. The house was sold.

6

Antiquing in Yucca Valley

Brian and Stéphane loved antiquing. Stéphane had an extensive collection of powder boxes, puffs, and compacts. Brian collected Carolyn Keene's Nancy Drew Mystery books and vintage salt and pepper shakers. John Spinney, the guard on the gate at Twilight Manors, recommended they drive up to the high desert, to a strip of storefronts in Yucca Valley, about thirty miles north of Palm Springs. He described it as "a bunch of stores run by geriatric hippies."

After lunch, with Stéphane in the passenger seat, Brian drove out of Palm Springs toward Desert Hot Springs, a predominantly Mexican town north of Palm Springs. Brian fixated on Alice and Jennie's long-haired, one-eyed chihuahua. "I think Mitzi has it in for me. I know that chihuahuas are temperamental, but that dog is possessed, a demon dog summoning the wrath of Lucifer down upon me. I wouldn't be surprised if one night I wake up and find myself floating downstream in a river of fire and blood, getting my face pecked off by pterodactyls. It'll be a cross between *Jumanji* and *Jurassic Park*."

"Brian, don't you think you might be overstating it slightly? Just a little bit."

"No, I don't. Mitzi is the Adolf Hitler of the chihuahua world. Give her half a chance, and she'll invade Poland."

"Brian, Mitzi weighs 3lbs. She might even be docile now she's been tased. By docile, I mean brain damaged. She probably doesn't even know what day of the week it is."

"Dogs rarely, if ever, know what day of the week it is. Most canines are baffled by calendars. Did you ever see a dog with a datebook? Ask a poodle what they have planned for next Wednesday, and they'll look at you as if you're an idiot. That's why Mitzi is such a freak. It's as if she *knows* something."

"Enough about that damn dog. Today we're having a quiet and peaceful day out. It'll be nice to get out of Palm Springs and the heat."

The temperature was ninety-five degrees, cool for the summer in Palm Springs. Brian drove with the windows down—he preferred fresh air. He knew that in the high desert, it would be ten degrees cooler. Stéphane stared out the window at the desert, and the mountains up ahead. "Some people have seen spaceships landing out here. Little green men with stalky eyes. Gender non-specific aliens covered in tin nipples and a circus of genitals. Blobs with goo-goo eyes and sparks instead of hair. You know the type."

"You don't believe in spaceships, do you?" Brian scoffed at the idea. "It's ridiculous. Why would intelligent life from another planet land here on Earth, a place where Barry Manilow passes for entertainment."

"I thought we'd agreed to never mention Barry Manilow ever again. He's mediocre and lame."

"I'm sorry, Stéphane, his name slipped out. I'll never mention him again. I promise." Brian suppressed a smile.

"To answer your question, no, I don't believe in little green men from Mars. But I do wonder why people *say* they've seen spaceships."

"To make themselves feel *special*, that they have been *chosen*, or maybe they really can see something that most of us can't see—either because they're hallucinating, on drugs, or they're completely insane."

"Some claim to have been abducted and had medical experiments performed on them, like being anally probed. That's a laugh. You don't have to board a spaceship to get anally probed. Not in Palm Springs, anyway. You can get anally probed at any time of the day. Anywhere—

even up against a dumpster at the back of In-N-Out Burger or by five guys at Five Guys. I remember growing up in the 1960s at the height of alien abductions. The papers were full of it. People were getting beamed up willy-nilly all over the place."

"Yes, I remember that too. I blame *Star Trek*. That started in 1966 and ended in 1969. That was the time frame of most alien abductions."

Stéphane shrugged. "You might be right about *Star Trek*. I wouldn't mind being anally probed by a young Captain Kirk. He was my first crush. And Klingons. I had the hots for Klingons. I can even speak a little Klingon. ... mumuSHa'."

"What does that mean?"

"It means 'make love to me.' I learned it in case I ever ran into a hot Klingon in the supermarket. I also speak Swedish Chef. 'Foockcken me in der ass.' It means the same thing."

"Yes, I got that one. My first TV crush was Robert Conrad in *The Wild Wild West*. His shirt flew off in virtually every episode. Did he even own a shirt? And Howdy Doody."

"Howdy Doody?"

Brian shifted in his seat. "And Lambchop, the sheep who was fisted by Shari Lewis. And Fred Flintstone—he was hot in that animal print mini dress with the cravat. I pretended I was Wilma Flintstone wearing that off-the-shoulder number she always wore and the white rock necklace. I used to jerk off waiting for Fred to come home from work at the Slate Rock and Gravel Company."

"I wanted to be Agnes Moorehead in *Bewitched*."

Brian slowed down as he reached a T junction. "I think we turn right here by the water tower and head for those mountains."

They drove up the winding road through Morongo Valley. Soon they were in the high desert, driving through small communities with broken-down houses, feed stores, Joshua trees, seedy saloons, and cactus farms. Another few miles and Brian pulled over. "Here it is."

"That one looks interesting." Stéphane pointed and climbed out of the car. "Let's go in there first."

"Welcome to the Hoof and Saddle Vintage Clothing Store." The elderly woman behind the counter put down her knitting and smiled as the two entered. "Welcome. Is this your first visit?" She wore a hairband holding back an unruly hedge of gray hair. Her eyes sparkled like diamonds.

"Yes. We moved to Palm Springs quite recently. This is our first visit to Yucca Valley." Brian eyed a beige cowboy hat balanced precariously on a Styrofoam head. "Stéphane, look at this, a real Stetson cowboy hat with a snakeskin hatband."

"That's a sheriff's hat from the 1950s. Gene Autry, the singing cowboy, had one just like it. It's easy to imagine him wearing it in *The Big Sombrero*, riding across the desert, and singing 'You Belong to My Heart.'" The woman took the hat, placed it on her head, and sang, "*'Twas a moment like this. Do you remember? And your eyes threw a kiss. When they met mine. Now we own all the stars, and a million guitars are still playing. Darling, you are the song, and you'll always belong to my heart.*"

Brian tried on the hat. It was too big. "Honestly, I don't think I'm the cowboy type. I wish I was, but I'm not. I grew up in Lowell, Massachusetts, not known for cowboys. The nearest I got to cowboys was watching *Bonanza* and *Rawhide* with Clint Eastwood. And *Wagon Train*. Did you know that Bette Davis appeared as a guest star in three episodes of *Wagon Train*? I only know that because we were born in the same town, as was Jack Kerouac. Unfortunately, he wasn't in *Wagon Train*."

Stéphane laughed. "I'm convinced that every second, somewhere in the world, a homosexual mentions Bette Davis."

"Or Joan Crawford."

"Let me try it on." Stéphane slid the hat onto his head. He looked in the mirror. "Very *Brokeback Mountain*. It fits, but it's not me, is it?"

"No, Stéphane, you need a smidge of masculinity to get away with wearing a cowboy hat. And you don't have that smidge. Not even a fraction of a smidge. And you're not butch enough to be a cowgirl. Have you considered that red ballgown over there? That's more your thing."

Stéphane's eyes lit up. "Oh, it is fabulous." He took the dress from the hanger, held it up to his body, and admired himself in the mirror. "I love it, the only problem is that it hides my beautiful Betty Grable legs. Over the years, many people have said I have her gams."

"Not when she was alive. You might have her legs the way they look now since she's been dead since 1973. But in other ways, it suits you. Those gray squiggly bits highlight your facial laugh line—wrinkles."

Stéphane ignored him. "Her legs were insured for $1 million. I should insure mine."

They left the Hoof and Saddle Vintage Clothing Store with two Marabou feather fans. Next door was the Fairy Antiques and Curios Emporium, where an older man with waist-length white hair sat behind a desk. "Welcome to Fairy Antiques. My name's Gay Gandalf—like in Lord of the Cock Rings—just whistle if you need any help. You know how to whistle, don't you boys? You put your lips together and blow. Are you looking for anything in particular?"

"I collect powder puffs, boxes, and compacts." Stéphane cast his eyes around the store.

"We have a few in that cabinet next to the walking sticks. I know there's a 1930s Bakelite powder puff musical trinket box there."

Brian made his way to DISCO CORNER, an area of albums by Sylvester, Sister Sledge, Chic, Village People, posters, and books. "Stéphane, we must buy this Divine *Lust in the Dust* poster for the guest bathroom."

"For sure." Stéphane scanned the powder puff cabinet, but there was nothing there to excite him. Then out the corner of his eye, he saw a book propped up on a shelf between a pair of porcelain King Charles spaniels. It was *The Donna Reed Show Pictorial Memoir*.

"Look at this, Brian. You don't think about Donna Reed for years, and then, suddenly, she's following us around. It's only $15. I'm buying it for the coffee table. It goes with the Tom of Finland books, the *Victoria Principal Workout Book*, Maureen Gilmer's *Palm-Springs-Style Gardening,* and that pop-up penis book called *Dicks Ahoy*."

It was late afternoon when they decided to stay for an early dinner in Yucca Valley before driving back down the mountain to Palm Springs. The only café on the strip was the Dippy Hippy Vegan Café. There was a small patio area with a few bedraggled customers and their mongrels on rope leashes. Patchouli hung in the air like mustard gas.

"Brian, there seems to be a lack of hairbrushes in Yucca Valley. As a result, everyone's hair looks like macrame—remember those three-tier macrame plant holders back in the 1970s?"

"Ugly, ugly, but we all had them, didn't we?"

Inside the Hippy Dippy Vegan Café, more customers were seated at park benches in a large room, reading or working on laptops. The walls were adorned by the work of local artists. Stéphane and Brian both ordered the tofu "egg" wrap.

They sat at a table outside. Five minutes later, a young woman brought their wraps. Stéphane bit into his. "It's delicious. I like vegan food, but I don't think I could go vegan. I'd miss bacon."

"So would I. You know, Stéphane, it's been a good day. No floaters in the pool, no sitting on cactuses, just a restful day. I think I'm getting used to living here in the desert. The key is not to try but just relax and allow things to happen on their own. Don't rush anything."

"I love it here in Yucca Valley. It's a million miles away from our life in Chicago. That *Lust in the Dust* poster was a find. Remember when we saw Divine performing in that club in Chicago? That was sometime back in the early 1980s. Great times."

"Divine was great. But that night was a disaster. Remember those pills I bought? I thought they were Quaaludes. You wouldn't take any. You said you had to work the next day. Wise choice, as it turned out, they were a horse laxative. Fast-acting, too. That was the one, and only time I pooped five times my own weight."

Stéphane cringed at the memory. "Right there on the disco floor, if I remember correctly. Right in the middle of "Hold Me Now" by the Thompson Twins. Then I managed to get you out of the club and into that back alley."

"Oh, Stéphane, that was not my finest hour. I shudder to think about it. And when I squatted by the Dumpster, who knew a homeless man was sleeping there? I certainly didn't. He should have said something. If I woke up and found someone pooping on my head, I'd say something. Wouldn't you?"

"I certainly would. But luckily, it didn't really matter, as the guy had overdosed. He was as stiff as a board. Dead as a doornail."

"Yes, I remember you called the police anonymously, and then we got out of there." Brian stopped when a young man walked into the café with a monkey on his shoulder.

"He's adorable. Is he friendly?" Stéphane was smitten with the cute monkey. "What's her name?"

"She's called Donna Reed. That's what my grandmother calls her. It's her monkey. I don't know if Donna Reed is a real person or whether she made her up. I've never heard of her."

Brian looked at Stéphane. Stéphane looked at Brian.

As they descended the winding mountain road back to Palm Springs, the sun began to set over the mountains. Brian pulled the car over onto the desert. "Stéphane, let's watch the sun go down. It'll be like we're riding off into the sunset together. I'll be Butch Cassidy, and you can be the Sundance Kid."

"Butch? You—butch!"

"Ok, we're two Sundance Kids."

The two men walked out into the desert, held hands, and watched as the sun set behind the mountains. Brian squeezed Stéphane's hand. "This has been a perfect day. Peaceful. No floaters in the pool, no parking my ass on a cactus, no ABBA clogs. You know that I love you, don't you? More than anything else in the world. Even though you're an idiot sometimes."

"I love you too, Brian. You can't help it that you're a fuckwad."

7

At the Supermarket

Brian parked the car outside of Von's supermarket. He and Stéphane were on a tight schedule; the post office closed at 4 o'clock, and they had groceries to pick up first. Brian pushed the cart up the liquor aisle. "Let's get a bottle of Belvedere vodka." Brian slipped the vodka into his cart. "Stéphane, you go and get the vegetables. I'll focus on the dairy. We need to power-shop."

Stéphane disappeared. Brian read the label on a carton of strawberry yogurt. He had lost many battles in his lifelong war against flab. But he hadn't lost the war itself. The war continued. Yogurt is what he should be eating. He knew that. But temptation lay everywhere. A carton of rice pudding whimpered quietly to itself on a nearby shelf, "Eat me, eat me." But Brian knew that the rice pudding with its yummy sugariness was tricking him. "Eat me, eat me." The rice pudding's voice was low and masculine, sensual, drawing him into its web. If the rice pudding had been a man, he would be muscular, strong, and hung like a horse. A manly rice pudding. Brian was weak-willed. He felt himself falling into the vortex of delicious, fattening foods. Brian looked around him—the coast was clear, so he licked the rice pudding's plastic container. The rice pudding spoke, "Oh, you want me, don't you, Brian? You want to push your tongue deep into my creamy pudding?" Brian closed his eyes and attempted to pull himself together. Rice pudding is a gateway drug. What next? Peanut butter? Chocolate cake? Krispy Kreme donuts? Brian's willpower was on the brink of collapse when his thoughts were interrupted by a voice. "Oh, don't buy that one. This one is much healthier." A man with graying tousled curls held out another brand of strawberry yogurt. "I'm sorry, I shouldn't be intruding. But that yogurt has been taken off the shelves in most supermarkets. Botulism. My name's Erik Riverlight." The two men shook hands. "I'll be moving to Palm Springs soon."

"Where are you from?"

"Portland, Oregon."

"I'm Brian. We moved here from Chicago. We haven't been here long either."

"We?"

"Yes, my husband, Stéphane, is over there in the fruit and veg department. You'll love living here in Palm Springs. It's very peaceful and relaxing."

Erik smiled sweetly. "That's why we're moving here, for the peace and quiet. Living in a bigger city is stressful."

"But isn't Portland peaceful? I always imagine it as a place where young men are busily growing their beards, and young women dye their hair blue and eat vegan minestrone soup."

Erik laughed. "Yes, it is a bit like that. My wife and I—my wife's name is Heather—we plan to open a meditation school. We don't know anyone here. Perhaps when we settle in, you and your husband could visit us for tea. We're planning on building a Zen garden and teahouse."

Brian was already conjuring up excuses to get out of it. A selection ran through his mind. *I'm so sorry but we have a previous engagement that day. A bar mitzvah.* Or what about, *I'm sorry we can't come on that day, Stéphane is having his hysterectomy.* Brian and Stéphane were not the "drinking tea in a Zen garden" type. They were more the drinking gin and falling over type. Brian and Stéphane were the kind of couple who, if they moved in next door to you, your lawn would die. They did not blossom in polite society. Erik Riverlight had "polite society" written all over him.

Brian took Erik's suggested yogurt and placed it in his cart. "I think you'll find that Palm Springs is the perfect place for your meditation center. Not much happens here."

Their conversation was interrupted by a gut-wrenching scream. Brian recognized the voice. He ran to the vegetable and fruit department, where Stéphane was throwing cans of peaches at the bananas. "Stéphane, what's wrong?"

"It came out of the bananas. It's crawling."

"Stéphane, calm down. You're getting hysterical."

"It was big and hairy, and I'm afraid of it."

There was no consoling him, so Brian slapped Stéphane hard across the face. "Now, calm down and tell me what happened."

A shop assistant intervened. "Hey, stop hitting that man. Are you alright, sir?" She stood between Brian and Stéphane. "Hit him again, and I'll call the police."

Stéphane grinned. "He's always hitting me like that. He won't stop. I'm an abused woman. Just kidd—"

Stéphane was interrupted by a woman screaming. "A spider! It's a tarantula. It's crawling over the cumquats."

"I told you there was something hairy in the bananas." Stéphane buried his face in his hands. "Brian, you know I'm terrified of spiders. Remember when you took me to see that old sci-fi movie, *Tarantula,* and I threw up over that woman in the row in front of us."

"I remember the dry-cleaning bill and her date taking a swing at me. I remember the police being called. I remember being thrown into a cell."

Another gut-wrenching scream rent the air. A woman pointed. "It's over there."

Even Brian could see that this was no ordinary spider. It was the size of a fist and rattled by the barrage of canned peaches. Moreover, this spider was in a bad mood. The woman fainted and knocked over a display of oranges. They rolled across the supermarket floor, adding to the chaos. The tarantula dashed for cover. A young boy tried to step out of the way of the rolling oranges. Instead, he stepped on one and skidded into a display of donuts and crullers. Stéphane picked up a bottle of soy sauce and slung it at the spider who was now hiding by the leeks. The bottle smashed. A young woman with a stroller ran for cover.

The manager appeared from his office. "What's going on here?" He was hit in the head with a jar of strawberry jam, and he dropped to the floor, bleeding from an open wound. Stéphane made a dash for the bakery, followed by the spider who appeared to be chasing him. Or so Stéphane thought. Stéphane ran behind the counter, panicked, and dived into the cake display case, crushing them all. "Help! Help!"

The two women behind the bakery counter made a dash for the exit. One got out. The other slipped on a broken jar of mayonnaise and cracked her head on a free-standing display of Coco Pops. The pyramid of boxes tumbled. A man appeared from the frozen food aisle. He was nudging sixty years of age. He was wearing Lycra shorts, a tight tank top reading "Let's Be Gay, Let's Be Gay, Let's Be Gay," and enough eyeshadow to paint a wall mural in a downtown strip mall. "What's happening here? This looks like fun."

Stéphane, still prostrate in the cake display, pointed to the tarantula. "The spider."

The man in the Lycra shorts screamed, picked up a jar of marmalade and threw it at the cabbages.

Brian grabbed his arm. "What did you do that for?"

"I don't know. I just got sucked up into the drama of it all."

Leslie—her badge read—a checkout girl trapped the tarantula in the pasta aisle. She surrounded it with jars of tomato sauce, then laid out boxes of spaghetti on the top like a lid. "I've caged it."

Two ambulances and a cop car pulled up outside the supermarket. Stéphane climbed out of the display case. He was covered in cake and cream and had a cherry balanced on top of his head. A strand of marzipan hung from one ear.

"Yes, that's him." A shop assistant pointed at Brian. "He's the spousal abuser. He's been abusing that man over there, the one covered in cream with a cherry on his head. I saw him slap that man."

There was another scream as an even bigger tarantula crawled out of the bananas. A policeman saw the spider and jumped into the plums with a loud squish. "Look at the size of that thing."

Another policeman pulled out his gun and shot at the second spider, shattering a display case containing mixed green salad, baby spinach, and some reasonably priced and delicious-looking chocolate parfait. Other customers rushed out of the store.

Brian struggled as he was handcuffed by the police and dragged out of the store. After being shoved into the police car, Brian saw Erik Riverlight, covered in what looked like body wash or shampoo. "Hi Erik, welcome to Palm Springs. Good luck with the Zen garden—it's very peaceful here. Nothing much happens."

A man ran out of the store pushing a shopping cart filled with Johnny Walker Black Label cases. He disappeared across the parking lot. Then he loaded up a truck and drove off.

"They're looting the place." A cop threw up his hands. "I give up."

Stéphane tried to pull Brian out of the police car. "That's my husband. Let him go."

"Back away, sir. This man is being arrested for domestic violence."

Another ambulance pulled up. A bedraggled policeman emerged from the store. He was holding the harness of a seeing-eye dog. A steak hung from its jaws. "Does this dog belong to anyone?" There was no answer. "Okay, listen up, we've lost a blind person somewhere in the store."

Another cop took the dog. "What does this blind person look like?"

"How do I know what they look like? They're blind. Even they don't know what they look like." The second cop was then hit in the head by a can of chickpeas.

Suddenly, a screaming woman ran out of the store, across the parking lot, body-slammed a palm tree, and passed out cold. The chaos was spreading.

Brian and Stéphane never made it to the post office.

8

Satori

At breakfast the following morning, Brian sipped his iced coffee. "I think you outdid yourself yesterday at the supermarket. You caused total mayhem. This was better than that time you found a cockroach in your chocolate croissant in that Swedish bakery in Chicago."

"That wasn't my fault."

"You punched the waiter in the face."

"I stood up, and my hand brushed against him. That's not the same as punching someone in the face. And I never saw the old lady in the wheelchair. And I certainly never threw that rumball at her."

"Apparently, they were picking chocolate sprinkles out of her hair for a week. But yesterday at the supermarket, Stéphane, you truly surpassed all your previous disasters. One of your finest moments."

"There's no need to be sarcastic. You know I don't like spiders. Or any creepy crawlies, for that matter, and I include politicians and lawyers in that group. And people who do jigsaw puzzles, they give me the creeps."

"Stéphane, you wrecked the place. A whole supermarket. They had to close it down after the power was cut."

"That wasn't my fault. The police cut the power when they saw sparks coming out of the freezer—pizza section, I believe."

"It doesn't matter what section it was."

"No, wait a minute, it wasn't the pizza section. It was in the ice cream section."

"Stéphane, it doesn't matter where the sparks were coming from, they shut off the power, and all the meat was spoiled. Not to mention everything else. It was mass hysteria on a massive scale. The police are still looking for the looters."

"If they'd checked the bananas for spiders before putting them out on the stand, none of this would have happened."

"The tarantulas weren't brought in on the bananas. They were deliberately put there to cause panic and mayhem. It was a shoplifting gang. They've been pulling this stunt all over California."

"That can't be true. How much money can you make shoplifting from a supermarket?"

"After you screamed that first time, dozens of flash mob looters loaded their carts with liquor and anything else they could grab and ran out."

Brian and Stéphane were arrested outside the supermarket but were released—once the police found out that Brian wasn't a "wife" beater and Stéphane wasn't the leader of a shoplifting gang. Unfortunately for Erik Riverlight, he was charged with shoplifting after running from the chaos holding a six-pack of strawberry yogurt. The headline on the front page of the *Desert Sun* read, "Spider Panic Shuts Down Supermarket."

Brian scooped a spoonful of scrambled eggs onto his plate. "I wonder when we get to meet the new owners of Grahame's house. I haven't heard any noise coming from next door. Nothing."

"I wonder what happened to Mistress Rosemary and her diaper boys. There was nothing in the paper about the drowned Jehovah's Witness with the ball gag and handcuffs. You'd think that would be a spicy story, but nothing. It's a mystery. Hey Brian, there's an update on the Donna Reed pubic wig story. This Donna Reed story isn't going away."

"What's happened now?"

"Did you know she once lived here in Palm Springs?"

"No, but it's not entirely surprising. So that's why the *Desert Sun* is milking this story. Any Hollywood-connected story and this town goes apeshit. 'Doris Day's hairdresser loses purse in Walgreens.' Harpo Marx's grandson eats his mother's hamster.' It's hardly big news, is it? Some old TV actress's merkin goes missing. I don't think we're witnessing the downfall of western civilization."

Stéphane shook the creases out of the paper and folded it in half. "Donna Reed lived at 1184 Cam Mirasol, that's over in north Palm Springs."

"What do they say about the pubic wig?"

"Apparently, the wig is only the latest in a long line of Donna Reed memorabilia thefts. It says here that someone tried to steal her Oscar for Best Supporting Actress in *From Here to Eternity* last year. It was in the historical museum in Denison, Iowa. Apparently, she was born there. The thief was interrupted by a security guard and made a run for it. If it's the same thief who stole the pubic wig, they must be a hardcore Donna Reed fan?"

"Does Donna Reed have hardcore fans?"

Stéphane stiffened. The blood drained from his face.

"What's wrong? You've gone as white as a ghost."

"I've just experienced satori. Sudden illumination."

"Stéphane, what are you talking about?"

"I don't believe it. Remember the day we went to the 'Movie Accessories' exhibit at the Palm Springs Museum? Remember when we were standing outside—"

"—And you were tripping people up."

"Before that. That first guy that bumped into me, the guy that worked in the ice cream parlor."

"What about him?"

"Remember he was wearing a fake goatee that was falling off. That was—"

"—No!"

"Yes!"

"No!"

"Yes, that phony goatee was Donna Reed's pubic wig. He was stealing it."

A wave of realization passed over the breakfast table. A wave so high, the Beach Boys could surf on it. Brian's jaw dropped. A minute or two passed, then Brian broke the silence. "So, the guy from the ice cream parlor snatched Donna Reed's pubic wig from the display case, stuck it on his chin, and walked out of the museum. Unnoticed, except by us."

"It certainly looks that way."

"How do you feel about going for ice cream today?"

"Sounds like an excellent idea."

9
Following Jed

At the Cold Comfort Shake Rattle and Roll Ice Cream Parlor, the young man they saw running from the Hollywood Accessories exhibition stood behind the counter taking orders. His name badge read "Jed." Brian and Stéphane ordered their usual Almond Joy shake and a Key Lime Pistachio cone. They sat on their regular stools in the window.

Brian sucked on his Almond Joy. "He doesn't look the type to steal a pubic wig."

"What do pubic wig thieves look like?"

"No, Stéphane, what I meant was that he doesn't look old enough to even remember Donna Reed. How old is he? Thirty maybe. He wasn't even born when Donna Reed died. I think we're barking up the wrong tree here. I think if he stole a pubic wig, it would be Taylor Swift's or Adele's or Beyonce's or Kim Kardashian's. Or whoever else is the flavor of the month."

"Ok, if you were going to steal a celebrity's pubic wig, who would it be?"

Brian thought for a moment. "First off, I can't believe we're having this stupid conversation. But—I'd go for Channing Tatum. Whose pubic wig would you choose?"

"I'd say Johnny Depp or James Franco. You know, bad boy pubic wigs."

Brian laughed. "I thought you were going to say, Nancy Pelosi."

"Why would I say, Nancy Pelosi? Why would I want Nancy Pelosi's pubic wig, for god's sake? Maybe she's got a Brazilian, a landing strip."

"I heard that Mother Theresa had a Brazilian."

"Now that, I can believe. She didn't fool me with all that nice-nun crap. If you look deep into Mother Theresa's eyes, you'll find a hot-blooded woman just gagging for a man's love. Or a woman's love. Or Barry Manilow's love."

The smile disappeared from Brian's face. "I thought we agreed that we would never mention Barry Manilow's name again. I don't like his music, and I don't like him."

"Sorry, Brian, it slipped out."

They were interrupted by Jed behind the counter calling to another worker. "Lunchbreak. I'll be back in an hour. I need to run home quickly."

Brian and Stéphane left the ice cream parlor and waited on the corner. A minute or so later, Jed appeared and headed off down the street in the opposite direction. Brian and Stéphane followed from a safe distance. They lost him briefly, then picked him up again and trailed him for three short blocks. Finally, Jed turned into the driveway of a beautiful mid-century modern house.

Stéphane nodded toward the opposite side of the street. "There's a Starbucks. Let's go for coffee. We can see when he leaves. That's if we're not banned. For some reason, you always make a scene in Starbucks."

"The people who work at Starbucks are assholes. And the people who sit there on their laptops are like zombies. The zombie apocalypse has already happened. If you don't believe me, go to a Starbucks near you."

Stéphane sighed. "Here we go again."

Brian and Stéphane sat in the window. Stéphane sipped his iced coffee. "That was weird up in Yucca Valley, wasn't it? Who would call their monkey Donna Reed? I wonder if the monkey had anything to do with the pubic wig going missing. Maybe the monkey broke into the museum in Iowa and tried to steal Donna Reed's Oscar, like the murderous orangutan in *The Murders in the Rue Morgue* by Edgar Allan Poe. Or maybe it's like the musical *Oliver … Why should we all break our backs? Better pick-a-pocket or two …* Maybe there's a Fagin somewhere with a posse of thieving monkeys. Or maybe he's one of the flying monkeys in *The Wizard of Oz.*"

"I doubt it. I admit that I looked to see if the monkey in Yucca Valley was wearing a pubic wig."

Stéphane laughed. "So did I?"

"That's something that never happened in Chicago. When we lived there, we never checked out the pubic wig status of monkeys. We were too busy shoveling snow. Although, I do remember the incident with the sock monkey."

"I'd forgotten all about that. It appeared on our doorstep with a note attached, 'For Stephanie,' and we thought it said, 'For Stéphane.' And you gave the sock monkey away to Goodwill. It turned out that it was a gift for the little girl next door, Stephanie. And the neighbors accused us of stealing a little girl's sock monkey. Made a big fuss about it. There was no need to get the police involved. I wonder where Stephanie is now."

"In therapy somewhere. Losing a sock monkey is like losing a parent. You never get over a thing like that. That's a burden you carry until the day you die. Nobody should have to lose a child or a sock monkey." Brian broke his banana and walnut muffin in half. "So, what's the plan?"

Stéphane thought for a moment. "Let's just take a look at the house."

"There might be someone there. Who says Jed lives alone?"

"If anyone comes to the door, we'll say we're Mormons."

"Aren't we a bit old to be Mormon missionaries? Aren't they all twenty years old, blond-haired, dumb, and full of cum? And they always wear black suits and ties. Here we are in jeans and T-shirts. You're T-shirt says 'Pink Floyd.' I don't think Joseph Smith had much to say about Pink Floyd."

"Do you have a better plan? I'd love to hear it. I'm waiting."

Brian shrugged. "No, I guess I don't."

"Then we'll say we're Mormons."

"What if they ask us in? We don't know anything about being Mormon."

Stéphane laughed. "What's there to know? They wear magic underwear."

"What does that look like?"

"You know, ugly underwear." Stéphane was losing his patience.

"Like those boxer shorts you bought me last Christmas."

"They weren't ugly."

"They had Christmas elves on them indulging in sadomasochism. Talk about bad taste. It ruined my Christmas, not to mention Jesus' birthday. There was a fisting scene around my crotch area."

"I thought you might find them erotic. I was trying to spice up our sex life."

"The only thing that would spice up our sex life is if you got out the bed and Idris Elba climbed in. I know this will amaze you, Stéphane, but I don't get turned on by elves urinating on each other. Also, call me old-fashioned, but the nipple clamps on Mrs. Claus crossed a line. What else do we know about Mormons?"

"We saw Donny Osmond in *Joseph and the Amazing Technicolor Dreamcoat*. Also, we saw *The Book of Mormon*."

"I love that musical. Especially the song, 'Hasa Diga Eebowai.'" Brian began to sing in his best Ethel Mormon voice. "*Fuck you God in the ass, mouth and cunt-a ... Fuck you, God, in the ass, mouth and cunt-a ... Fuck you, God, in the ass, mouth and cunt-a ... Fuck you in the eye!*"

Stéphane joined in.

Outside on the sidewalk, Brian huffed. "*The Book of Mormon* opened directly on Broadway, for Christ's sake. It was a huge success, grossing over $500 million, which means we got kicked out of Starbucks for singing a hit Broadway tune. And in Palm Springs of all places! Fuck Starbucks. Fuck them in the ass, mouth, and cunt-a. If we'd sung 'Hello Dolly,' they probably would have lined us up against a wall and shot us. What does Starbucks have against Broadway musicals?"

"Brian, let it drop. Some people don't like the 'C' word. Some people think it's a derogatory word for lady-parts."

Jed appeared out of the driveway opposite, walked down the street, then turned a corner and was gone. He was headed back to the Cold Comfort Shake Rattle and Roll Ice Cream Parlor to finish his shift.

"Ok, Stéphane, let's put on our magic Mormon underwear and march over to the house like we're spreading the good word."

"And what is the good word?"

"The good word is supercalifragilisticexpialidocious."

10

Angelica Fosgrave

Stéphane and Brian walked down the short drive past an RV parked near
an untrimmed hedge of red bougainvillea. A tortoiseshell cat hissed and
scampered away into the bushes. At the front door, Brian pressed the
doorbell. There was no answer. Brian rang the bell again. Finally, it was
answered by a frail woman in her eighties. "Hello, can I help you?"

Brian smiled like a Mormon, his tombstone teeth gleaming in the
sunlight. "We're here from the Church of Latter-Day Saints. And we
would like to—"

"—Oh, please come in. I'd love to hear what you have to say. It gets
very lonely being an old woman, when all your friends are dead and gone.
The last one to go was Gladys. I met her in a Beatnik café in Los Angeles,
it must have been around 1960 ... had a parrot called Twizzle ... her
husband was an art dealer ... had an automobile accident around 1963 ...
died when her implants started leaking ... buried in Forest Lawn, near
Carole Lombard. Would you like some chamomile tea and cookies? Did
you say you were morons?"

Brian looked at Stéphane. Stéphane focused on a stone frog catching
a fly next to the front door. They didn't bother to correct her. They
followed the woman through a small hallway with shelves cluttered with
Hummel figurines and into a large lounge. "Please sit down. I've just
made a pot of tea." The woman disappeared into the kitchen. "Make
yourself at home."

Brian and Stéphane sank into a monstrous rust-colored velour sofa. It felt like it was eating them alive. The couch had depictions of a rustic cottage and a garden fountain over the back. On the coffee table in front of them sat a tomato pin cushion, a couple of knitting patterns, a pair of No 19 needles, and a baby's pink bodysuit. Heavy drapes hung in the window, bright orange to match the deep shag carpet. A trio of plaster mallards flew across the wall, the last one slightly askew as if clipped by a hunter. A collection of record albums was stacked against the wall in a corner, including Dean Martin, Peggy Lee, and the Ray Conniff Singers. Without even using the bathroom, it was certain there was a shag-rug toilet seat cover. The kitchen, which Brian and Stéphane could see through an open doorway, had a rooster motif on tea towels, wallpaper, and framed pictures. The table had a gray Formica top with a pattern of overlapping boomerangs.

The old woman returned with a tray of tea and a plate of homemade chocolate chip cookies. "My name is Angelica Fosgrave. And you?"

Brian cleared his throat. "My name is Isaiah, and this is my brother, Brigham Hartvigsen."

"What lovely names. I always invite morons in. My friend Marjorie used to like the morons too. She passed away a while back ... met her in 1963 ... her husband was a lawyer ... Marjorie lost one of her fingers in a woodchipper accident ... had two kids, Paul and Lucy ... Paul went on to be in a pop group ... Lucy moved to Las Vegas to be a showgirl ... married Tony Bennett's chauffeur ... fell off a horse and died when she landed on a rattlesnake. Marjorie loved morons. So, tell me about the history of your church. I love hearing that story."

Brian panicked. "Well, it was started by Joseph Smith, a known drunk and womanizer—"

Stéphane stepped in. "—Which God forgave him for, didn't he?"

"Oh yes, completely. Because God is very forgiving. I can't tell you how many times God has forgiven me. Because I have sinned. Oh boy, have I sinned. Sometimes several times a day with several different men."

"So, Brian, why don't you tell Angelica the story of our church."

"Oh yes. Anyway, Joseph Smith found some golden tablets that he read, and then they disappeared. Some people think the Bee Gees stole them."

"Oh, talking of golden tablets, I've forgotten tea plates for the cookies." Angelica struggled into the kitchen again.

"Bee Gees! Brian—Bee Gees! The Bee Gees stole the golden tablets! What are you talking about? Have you gone nuts?"

"I panicked! I get the Bee Gees and the Osmonds mixed up—they're all teeth. That's all I remember about them—teeth. She's old. I bet she never even noticed. She's as dotty as hell."

"She seems pretty sharp to me. Oh, and Brian, neither the Bee Gees nor the Osmonds stole the golden tablets. Neither did Iron Maiden or the Carpenters. The plates just disappeared on their own like magic. Almost as if they never existed in the first place. Which, of course, in the real world, they didn't."

Angelica returned with three tea plates. "I'm sorry about that, now tell me about Joseph Smith and the Bee Gees. I didn't know the Bee Gees were morons."

Stéphane stepped in. "Oh yes, Barry, Maurice, and Robin Gibb were big morons."

"How interesting. My son, Bruce, was a big Bees Gees admirer. Sadly, Bruce was called to heaven a while back. Fell off a ladder while putting up Christmas decorations. God works in mysterious ways, doesn't he?"

"Yes, she certainly does." Brian shifted in his seat. The sofa slowly devoured him like quicksand in a vintage cowboy movie.

"His son, Jed, my grandson, lives in the RV in the driveway. You've just missed him. He was here to make my lunch."

"Sounds like a nice boy." Brian sank further into the sofa.

"Oh, he's a lovely boy. Looks after his grandmother."

"Have you been living here long?"

"I moved here in 1966 for work. I was in Los Angeles before that."

"What kind of work did you do?

"I was a housekeeper. I was a friend of Shelley Fabares. She played Mary Stone in *The Donna Reed Show*. Had a big hit with *Johnny Angel*. After the show ended in 1966, Shelley recommended me to Donna Reed. So, I moved out here and worked for Donna Reed for four years until she moved away. I know what you're thinking. You thought Donna Reed did all her own housework. She was always vacuuming in pearls and heels. That was just on TV. She never vacuumed anything in her life. That was my job. I met and married my husband here in Palm Springs. He owned a couple of restaurants. Have you been reading about Donna Reed's intimate wig being stolen? Who would do a thing like that? It's terrible. I remember that wig. I had the job of washing it. I used to put it in the dishwasher with the pots and pans. Do you know about the Donna Reed Fan Club?"

Brian was intrigued. "No, do they have meetings?"

"Yes, 6:00 p.m. the second Tuesday of every month, at the Lonely Boner Café. I stopped going years ago. My legs aren't what they were. I had a few of my own personal mementos of Donna Reed here until the burglary when they went missing."

"What memories?" Brian lit up.

"I only took things they were throwing away. I'm not a thief. But I did keep a few things of hers. My most precious keepsake of Donna Reed was a squeezed-out tube of her Preparation H. She suffered terribly from piles. Also, some cotton earbuds I found in the trash. Anyway, they're gone now since the break-in. Funny, they never took anything else, though. Just the Donna Reed items."

"Did you call the police?"

"No, of course not. The police would think me very strange, taking things from Donna Reed's bathroom trash can. Jed told me they would laugh at me."

Brian stared at his shoes. Stéphane gazed out the window.

11
Nessun Dorma!

After swimming a few laps in the pool, Stéphane and Brian sat at the breakfast table. It was going to be a scorching hot day. Beams of sunlight shone through the palm fronds above their heads. Hummingbirds hovered around the bright red feeders, their wings thrumming, long beaks and tongues sucking up the sap. A baby jackrabbit skittered across the garden—a family of bunnies was nesting under bushes near the swimming pool equipment. Brian vacantly stared into space. He was thinking about their visit to Angelica Fosgrave, about Donna Reed's squeezed-out tube of Preparation H, and about their lucky escape from being devoured by a velour sofa. "Stéphane, what did you think of the Fosgrave woman yesterday?"

"Seems nice enough, but the Donna Reed connection was a surprise. First, we see her grandson snatch Donna Reed's pubic wig from the exhibition, then his grandmother tells us she used to work for her. Everywhere we go, we're bumping into Donna Reed. It's almost like she's haunting us. Calling us from beyond the grave."

"I know. I'll be honest, I don't know what to think. Stealing a celebrity's pubic wig is a petty crime—quite amusing when you think about it. But I can't help thinking there's something else going on. Something sinister."

"Brian, is that your women's intuition?"

"Could be. Oh, well, I'm sure the fog surrounding this mystery will clear soon. It always does in those Margaret Rutherford Agatha Christie movies. Anyway, did the mail come?"

"Yes. Bank statements, a 20% off coupon for Bed, Bath, and Beyond. Do we need a new soap dish?"

"Not really, no."

"What's this?" Stéphane tore open an envelope and removed a card with a black border. "You're not going to believe this. We've been invited to a funeral."

"Not another one. Who is it this time? They're dropping like flies."

"Elizabeth Taylor."

"What? She passed away years ago."

"It's a poodle called Elizabeth Taylor. She's being buried at the Rainbow Bridge Pet Cemetery." Stéphane grinned.

"I don't know a dog called Elizabeth Taylor. Who are the owners?"

"Jean and Jeff Kandinsky."

"Oh, I know who it is. It's that couple we met at the karaoke night at the Twilight Manors community hall. The night you ruined 'The Trolley Song.'"

"I didn't ruin the song. I'm sure Judy Garland would have loved my version."

"That poor woman was so jacked up on pills she wouldn't know a good rendition of the song if it jumped up and bit her in the face."

"I wouldn't diss Judy Garland. Not in this town anyway. That's like pissing on the blue suede shoes of the gay community."

"The woman was a junkie. Bring on Janis Joplin, Amy Winehouse, Whitney Houston. Oh, I'm so rich and successful that I'll kill myself with drink and drugs while the rest of you have to work a shitty 9-5 job for minimum wage. Boo fucking hoo."

"Brian, you're not very sympathetic, are you?"

"Sympathy is just a word between shit and syphilis in the dictionary."

Stéphane changed the subject. "Anyway, back to the dog funeral. I remember the Kandinsky's at that karaoke night. He sang, 'D.I.V.O.R.C.E.' and she sang, 'I Never Promised You a Rose Garden' ... I'm surprised they're still together."

"I think we should go to the funeral. I've never been to a dog funeral. What do you wear?"

"A dog collar, and I'll take you on a leash. You'd like that, Brian, wouldn't you? Or one of those leather pup hoods you see at Leather Pride. Or a pair of low-key Hush Puppies."

Stéphane and Brian heard a truck pull up in front of the house. It was the gardeners, Margarita, and Isabella. Margarita appeared first with a leaf blower strapped to her back. She resembled a giant snail in a 1950s sci-fi B movie. "Good morning. We are here to transform your yard into a paradise." Margarita sailed past them like a Spanish galleon bloated with gold doubloons. She was an imposing figure. Over six feet tall and built like a Russian tank.

"We're just finishing breakfast." Brian cleared away the plates. "I heard on the grapevine that you're an actor."

"And a stunt woman. I worked on *Game of Thrones*. I was Jason Momoa's stunt double. Lovely man. I worked with him on *Aquaman* as well, and I also played a triceratops in *Jurassic World: Fallen Kingdom*. My wife here, Isabella, is also an actor. She played a store assistant in *Bad Santa 2*, and last week she auditioned to play a dancing tampon in a Taiwanese commercial."

"It's because I'm so thin." Isabella smiled sweetly. "I can squeeze through a cat flap."

Brian composed himself. "That's a handy skill for a lesbian to have."

"It's on my resume." Isabella wasn't joking.

"Can I make some suggestions for your garden?" Margarita produced a pen and notepad.

"Yes, of course, we know very little about gardening." Brian sat back.

"This fence along the back here—it needs honeysuckles. Ten Plants. It will give you more privacy. Here I suggest a pigmy palm. Are you using this glory hole here? Because if you aren't, I suggest you put a flap on this side to close it up and a hinge so you can open it up to spy on the neighbors. I'm writing you a shopping list—ten honeysuckle plants, one pigmy palm, and two barrel cactuses. If you go to Martie's Gardening Center in Palm Desert, make your order, and we'll pick it up and plant everything for you. Tell Martie that Margarita and Isabella sent you. You also need to contact pest control. You've got fruit rats." Margarita pointed to shells of oranges hanging from the tree. "They're eating your fruit."

There was a shuffling noise next door, then muffled voices in Spanish. Brian peered through the glory hole. "Men are working there. Four of them."

Margarita peered over the fence. "They're stripping everything away. The lawn's coming up. Looks like the new owners are designing their garden from scratch. Probably the best idea as it was very neglected. Did anything happen about that Jehovah's Witness floater wearing handcuffs and a diaper?"

"We never heard another word about it."

"That's odd. You'd think the papers would have been all over that story."

Brian pulled into Martie's Gardening Center parking lot. It backed onto a mountain. In fact, if there were a landslide, Martie's Gardening Center would disappear. "Now, Stéphane, we are about to sail through uncharted seas. What we know about desert landscaping could be etched onto a fly's asshole. Actually, we know less than that. We know nothing—zero."

"We've got Margarita's list. That's all we need."

In the distance they heard a deep masculine voice singing. "*Nessun dorma! Nessun dorma! Tu pure, o Principessa Nella tua fredda stanza Guardi le stelle che tremano D'amore e di speranza!*"

Stéphane grabbed Brian's arm. "Oh my God! Can you see what I see? It's a disco ball in motion. It's Pavarotti in drag. It could be Divine."

A bald man was walking toward them between two rows of jasmine plants wearing a sequined ballgown, dangling earrings, and carrying pruning shears. He was over six feet tall and weighed 350lbs. "Good morning, gentlemen. Welcome to Martie's Gardening Center. I'm Martie. Obviously, as you can tell, I'm fabulous. I won't shake hands. I don't want to crush these cheap rings I'm wearing. What can I do for you? No, wait a minute, let me guess. Margarita sent you."

"How did you know?" Brian was surprised.

"She called me. Said there were two handsome men coming my way. And that doesn't happen very often, let me tell you. Not anymore. Of course, years ago, the men hovered around me like flies on shit. I was the belle of the ball. I was hung like a horse and had the legs of Cyd Charisse. An intoxicating combination, I think you'll agree. I had straight men cumming all over me. I was their gateway drug between marriage to a woman and full-blown screaming homosexuality. I was the bridge bringing them out into the life. Five minutes with me, and they never looked at a woman again. Anyway, that's my sex life in a nut sac. Me and Margarita go back a long way. We were both drag queen wrestling champions in a bar in Kansas City a few years back. I was Mikey the Asswrecker, and she was Killer Queen. Margarita was a drag queen lesbian wrestler. Did she give you a list?"

"Yes. Ten honeysuckle plants, one pigmy palm, and two barrel cactuses."

"Follow me." Martie headed off to Cactus Corner.

Brian was intrigued. "How long have you been here?"

"I opened the garden center about five years ago. Before that I was a singer. *Giunse alfin il momento Che godrò senz' affanno In braccio all'idol mio Timide cure uscite dal mio petto! A turbar non venite il mio diletto. O come par che all'amoroso foco L'amenità del loco, La terra e il ciel risponda.* Mostly opera, but I can rap—just kidding. Here are the barrel cactuses. Do you know what you're looking for?"

Brian threw up his hands. "Not a clue."

"Would you like me to pick the plants for you?"

"Would you?"

"Of course. You should come and see me at the White Swallow on Saturday nights. That's where I perform. I do a wonderful Peggy Lee. You should see my 'Fever'—I wear this fiery red sequined dress, and I sweat like a pig. I'm told that's how Peggy did it, a bit of glam and sweating like a pig. But, of course, she was a terrible lush. That's something else we have in common. I'm in recovery myself. That's how my singing career ended. I was playing the Duke of Mantua in Verdi's *Rigoletto*. I was halfway through 'La donna è mobile,' when I fell into the orchestra pit onto a violinist. She was eating a sandwich at the time. She choked and died. I got three years in the slammer for involuntary manslaughter. Suddenly opera was in the rear-view mirror for me. But no matter. I'm happy here working with these beautiful plants." Martie hiked up his ballgown and scratched his blubbery fat bare ass. "As long as I can bring a little beauty into the world, I'm happy."

12
Goodbye Elizabeth Taylor

The pet cemetery was hidden behind a tall hedge at the end of a cul-de-sac. At the entrance, there was an archway with lettering that read, The Rainbow Bridge Pet Cemetery. Stéphane and Brian parked, then walked across a gaily painted rainbow bridge over a stream that skirted the perimeter of the burial ground like a moat around a castle. Row upon row of neat white headstones marked the love between humans and their pets. One read, "For Benny, a much-loved parakeet." Another, "Doris the Dormouse Gone to Heaven." Hidden speakers quietly played Johann Sebastian Bach's "Sheep May Safely Graze." A crowd of mourners gathered outside a small chapel. Jean and Jeff Kandinsky welcomed the guests. Stéphane took Jean's hand. "Brian and I were so sorry to hear about your loss."

"Thank you so much." Jean dabbed at her eyes with a handkerchief. "Yes, we miss her. Her little wet nose. The way she used to chew on Jeff's underwear and pee in his shoes. Little things like that are what you miss the most. Do you have any pets of your own, Brian?"

"Not since Stéphane's tropical fish drowned back in Chicago with the help of Windex."

"It's heartbreaking when you lose a much-loved pet."

"Yes, it is. I know that Elizabeth Taylor is irreplaceable, but perhaps you may find another poodle that needs a loving home one day."

"Oh no, never. I can't see anyone taking her place."

"Maybe a guinea pig or a stick insect."

"I don't see a guinea pig or a stick insect running to welcome me home when I get back from grocery shopping. I want a pet that I can cuddle."

"What about a hermit crab?"

The chapel was packed to the rafters. In Palm Springs, funerals are almost as common as staph infections. A woman at the door handed out programs and a plastic dog's head cone. "The bereaved have asked all the guests to wear dog head cones. I know it's a little unusual, but it's an homage to Elizabeth Taylor, who wore one to stop her biting her own stitches." The pet cemetery worker was visibly embarrassed but soldiered on. "Apparently, she was wearing a dog head cone when she was struck down by the lawnmower. Didn't see it coming. The bereaved want us all to share that moment."

Brian was speechless. Stéphane wasn't. "It's no bother, Brian. My husband here wears one of these all the time to stop him from biting his own ass."

Brian fixed his gaze on a stained-glass window depicting a goldfish being carried up to heaven on the wings of a dove. At the altar, mourners lined up to view the body."

"Brian, do you think we should get in line?"

"To see a dead dog—I don't think so. I've seen enough roadkill, thank you very much."

"This isn't roadkill. This is lawnmower kill."

"I don't care if she drowned in a vat of rice pudding. I don't want to see a dead dog."

Stéphane and Brian clipped on their dog head cones and sat in the pews at the back of the chapel in case they had to make a run for it. Several of the residents of Twilight Manors were there, including Alice, Jennie, and Mitzi, their annoying chihuahua.

Brian nudged Stéphane. "I see Mitzi is here. That dog hates me. I don't think she's seen me yet. She's plotting to kill me. I know that. Obviously, she can't do it herself, as she's too small. But I know she's looking to hire an assassin, a contract killer. Chihuahuas are not to be trusted."

"Brian, we're being beckoned. Mr. Olson, that mortuary beautician, is here. I think he wants to talk to us. We had better go over."

Olson was standing near the altar wearing a dog head cone. "Good to see you again. Haven't seen you since Graham's memorial."

"I didn't know you knew the deceased." Brian smiled.

"I didn't, but the Kandinskys hired me to beautify Elizabeth Taylor."

Stéphane stiffened with excitement. "You're telling me you've made her up."

"Well, Jean and Jeff wanted her to look her best, given the unusual circumstances of her death. Would you like to see her? I think this is possibly my best work. As an artist, I mean. This could be my Mona Lisa. But you be the judge."

Brian was confused. "Why are there seven Scooby-Doo lunch boxes on the altar."

"They contain the remains of Elizabeth Taylor. Seven boxes. She died in a freak lawnmower accident. She was sliced into seven parts. The last lunch box is open, and that one contains her head."

Brian and Stéphane's jaws dropped when they peered into Scooby-Doo lunchbox No 7.

Olson beamed with pride. "What do you think? The Kandinskys wanted her made up to look like Elizabeth Taylor in *Cleopatra*. Golden-flecked electric blue eye shadow on her top eyelids and green paste on her lower eyes. Then a touch of black kohl on her eyelashes."

Stéphane gasped. "It's remarkable. You're a true artist Mr. Olson. You've made a dead toy poodle look like Elizabeth Taylor. They look identical, apart from the fact that the poodle had four legs and the actor had two. Presumably, Elizabeth Taylor, the actor, had two legs. I never actually met her. Or counted her legs. Although, she had two legs in *Lassie Come Home*. Lassie, of course, had four legs."

"Phenomenal! Breathtaking!" Brian was visibly shocked. "This dead poodle is a dead ringer for Elizabeth Taylor, the actor. Have you made up pets before?"

"Oh yes, and not just dogs. Why only last week I made a terrapin look like Ingrid Bergman."

Brian looked at his shoes. Stéphane stared at the ceiling.

After the viewing, the mourners sat quietly in the pews waiting for the service to begin. The Rev. John Hopperly, wearing a dog collar and a dog head cone, began his eulogy:

"Elizabeth Taylor was not just a poodle but a lesson in how to love. Nobody loved the Kandinsky's more than their little 'fooky wooky fluffball.' Their 'icky bicky puff bottom' was always waiting by the door for mommy and poppy to return home, where 'ickle bicky pookie boo' would jump around to greet them. Until one day, 'booby pop frissors' lay hidden in the long grass with the spinning blades of a lawnmower heading in her direction. What happened next shouldn't have happened to anyone. Especially a toy poodle—a toy poodle with a heart of gold and only seconds to live."

Stéphane and Brian stopped listening. The Rev. Hopperly's voice droned on as ambient noise.

"Little dinky poos lived her life like a candle in the wind. And now we will sing Elizabeth Taylor's favorite song, Celine Dion's 'My Heart Will Go On' from Titanic."

The congregation sang.

At the graveside, Brian eyed Mitzi in the arms of Alice. Mitzi stared back at him. If looks could kill, Brian would be lying in the shallow grave with Elizabeth Taylor. A gravedigger stood nearby, leaning against a tree, with a spade over his shoulder. He smiled at Brian, that knowing "I'm gay, you're gay" smile. The pastor made a short speech, and it was over. As the mourners trailed away from the grave, whispering amongst themselves, an eagle circled overhead. Brian turned back just in time to see the eagle swoop down, pick up the lunchbox containing Elizabeth Taylor's head, then fly away with it in its claws. Brian locked eyes with the gravedigger. They both smiled. The gravedigger then shoveled soil onto the remaining six Scooby-Doo lunch boxes."

Neither Brian nor the gravedigger told a soul about what happened. It was their little secret.

13

The Donna Reed Fan Club

At the breakfast table the following morning, Stéphane picked up the *Desert Sun*. "Brian, look at this. The police are now looking for a woman for the theft of Donna Reed's pubic wig. She's shown up on a security camera outside the Palm Springs Art Museum."

"Why do they think it's her?"

"A witness says this woman was acting suspiciously when looking at John Wayne's dildo. Apparently, she started bawling her eyes out."

"I have to admit that my eyes watered a bit when I saw it. Well, it was impressive. But then, everything about John Wayne was larger than life. Of course, there's another way of looking at it—she may have been distracting everyone's attention away from the real thief."

"I don't understand why they don't have cameras inside the building."

"They do, but they were disabled."

"That means the robbery was planned. Someone really wanted that pubic wig, but why? What use is it?"

Stéphane read on. "It says here that the theft may be linked to bank robberies throughout the Coachella Valley."

"I thought they were looking for a man for the bank robberies. We saw it on TV the other night. I suppose they could be a team, like Bonnie and Clyde."

Stéphane's eyes widened. He leaned into the paper. "They *were* looking for a man for the bank robberies, but now they're looking for a woman dressed as a man. A male impersonator."

"Run that by me again. I'm getting gender-confused. That happens a lot in the gay world."

"They think the bank robberies are being committed by a woman dressed as a man. And they think that same woman stole Donna Reed's pubic wig—when she was dressed as a woman."

"What makes the police think it's the same person?"

"They don't say."

Brian threw up his hands. "From the sound of it, the truth is that the police have no idea who is committing these crimes. They're grasping at straws."

They were interrupted by voices coming from next door. Brian pulled back the newly installed flap on the glory hole and peered through. "1 ... 2 ... 3 ... 4 ... there are ten men next door. Oh my God!"

"What is it, Brian?"

"One of them is bending over to pick something up. I can see butt crack."

"Where?" Stéphane pushed Brian aside and peered through the hole. "I see what you mean. That's a very nice butt crack. There's nothing more enticing than a man bending over and flashing his butt crack. It's a sideways smile. It says, 'Oh boy, am I pleased to see you.'"

"Stéphane, I didn't know you spoke butt crack."

"I'm fluent. Butt crack is the language of love."

"Not much use ordering food in a restaurant, is it?" Brian slapped his own wrist. "We shouldn't be treating these men as sexual objects. I'm suddenly overwhelmed with politically correct guilt." Brian pushed Stéphane aside. "Oh, look, there's another one. That's two—no, three butt cracks." Brian sank to the ground in a stupor. Swooning. He was now sitting with his back resting against the fence with his eyes closed. "There's something magical about a man bending over in front of you. It's almost spiritual. I think it's a sign from God himself. It's as if God is saying, 'I give this offering to you, this gift of a butt crack.' I truly believe that an exposed butt crack gives us a glimpse into a man's soul. You can tell a lot about a man when he bends over. It reveals his inner strength and yummy deliciousness."

Stéphane sighed. "I know. I think that every butt crack hides a portal, a hidden door beyond which there's a phantasmagoric world of unicorns, dragons, and pleasure. They say that if you push your way into a man's butt crack far enough, you will eventually find yourself standing in Narnia talking to a mouse."

Brian swooned. "I believe that."

"A man's butt crack is a place of mystery and adventure. Like Atlantis or El Dorado, a lost world, or anywhere in Montana. It wouldn't surprise me if the Loch Ness Monster lurked beyond a man's sphincter of love. It wouldn't surprise me at all."

Brian pushed Stéphane out of the way. "Oh my God, one of them is scratching his balls." Stéphane almost passed out. "There's nothing prettier than a man scratching his balls. It says a lot about a man. It says, 'I am a man, and I have itchy balls.'"

"Oh sister, ain't that the truth."

Back at the breakfast table, Brian sipped his iced tea. "Well, that was a nice little diversion first thing in the morning. I now know what they mean when they say, 'up at the crack of dawn.' So what's on the agenda today?"

"According to the calendar—Ha! The Donna Reed Fan Club meets today at 6:00 p.m. at the Lonely Boner Café. Should we go?"

"Do we have anything better to do?"

The Lonely Boner Café was a popular soup and salad restaurant on Palm Canyon Drive. Apart from an excellent menu, the attraction was the large garden at the back with tables and chairs. The sun was setting over the mountains, and candles flickered on each table. On a small stage, a young woman called Erin with flowing red Irish hair played the harp—

"My Wild Irish Rose" and "Garryowen"—with all the tinkling passion that Irish songs deserve. Stéphane and Brian each ordered parsnip soup and a simple green salad. They sat at a table next to six people in the garden, five men and one woman, all wearing Donna Reed wigs.

"I didn't even know this place existed. What a charming spot to come for dinner." Brian nodded toward the next table, where a heated discussion was taking place about Season 4 Episode 4 of *The Donna Reed Show.* It was, apparently, called "Mouse at Play."

"It was one of my favorite episodes." The only woman in the group adjusted her Donna Reed wig. "When Iris dyes her hair blond, Donna goes platinum. But then regrets it. She avoids Alex until she has time to change the color back. Cloris Leachman played Myra."

Brian leaned across. "I'm sorry, but I overheard your conversation, and I have to say that I'm a big Donna Reed fan."

"Then you've come to the right place." The man was in his late eighties. Stylishly dressed, shirt, jacket, and a yellow cravat—he looked like he was auditioning for a senior production of *Boys in the Band.* "This is the Palm Springs chapter of the Donna Reed Fan Club. We've been meeting here since January 1986, when she passed away. There used to be more of us, but people have drifted away over the years. Many have joined Donna Reed in the afterlife. I'm Don, by the way. This is Harold, Jimmie, Lorna, Michael, and Sammy. We're all original members."

Brian and Stéphane shook hands with everyone in the group.

Jimmie leaned forward, "As you can see, we are all men and women of a certain age. Donna Reed is all but forgotten now. The young generation don't even know who she was. We enjoy keeping her memory alive. She was such an inspiration to us all when we were young and finding our way in the world. Even now, after all these years, I still vacuum in pearls and heels."

Sammy added. "We all do."

The six members of the Donna Reed Fan Club nodded in agreement.

Brian stared into space. Stéphane cleared his throat and said nothing.

The soup and salad arrived. Brian tore open a packet of ranch dressing. "I would have thought there would be more young people here. The 1960s are looked at with much fondness by some in the young generation."

Lorna smiled. "Donna Reed allowed us a break free from all the troubles in our own lives. A little bit of fluff to take our minds off the Bay of Pigs, the Cuban Missile Crisis, and the Vietnam War. My father died in that war. Without him, my mother was never the same again. She became mentally ill. She used to wander the streets at night wearing nothing but a chemise and stilettos. It was her illness that drove her to become a Tupperware salesperson. So, growing up, we kids never saw her much. Tupperware was a brainwashing cult back then—still is. My mother was more interested in storing food items and stacking containers neatly than feeding us. When she died, I kept her ashes in a Tupperware container in the kitchen until my daughter added them, by mistake, to a soup she was making. They were sad times. That's why we all vacuum in heels and pearls like Donna Reed, to keep our spirits up."

Sammy interrupted. "We did have that one young man turn up a few months back. Blond kid with a dragon tattoo on his arm. What was his name?"

Lorna thought hard. "Jeb, wasn't it?"

"No, it was Jed, the same name as a cousin of mine." Jimmie buttered a roll. "He only came to one meeting. He wasn't really interested in the legend that is Donna Reed. More the price of her memorabilia. I think he was a dealer. He told me I could sell my Donna Reed memorabilia online. I told him I had a lot of her personal possessions that I'd collected over the years, including a hairbrush. He was particularly interested in that—the hairbrush. I told him I wouldn't sell it, and that was the end of it. Things got frosty, and he left in a huff."

Lorna started choking. When she didn't stop, Stéphane jumped into action. He lifted the woman up, spun her around, and performed the Heimlich maneuver on her. She looked like a rag doll having a stroke while being rear-ended by a sissy. Lorna turned blue, then coughed up half a grape tomato, followed by her dentures. Her false teeth arced through the air and landed at the feet of Barney, a slobbering Great Dane at the next table. The dog picked up the teeth and swallowed them. Then the dog started choking. It was a chain reaction. Stéphane lifted the dog up onto his back legs and performed the Heimlich maneuver on the Great Dane. He was cross-eyed throughout the whole procedure. Barney coughed up the dentures into Brian's parsnip soup.

Erin, the harpist, played "When Irish Eyes Are Smiling."

14
The Painting

At the breakfast table the following morning, Stéphane opened the *Desert Sun*. "Oh, look at this. You were right about the police not knowing what they're doing with this Donna Reed case. They thought the pubic wig was stolen by a woman who was also robbing banks as a man. Now they've changed their mind—they think it's a man robbing the banks and the same man dressing as a woman to steal the pubic wig."

Brian leaned back in his chair. "So now they think it's a man. That's interesting."

"It says here that the woman they were looking for, the one who was seen acting strangely, was eliminated from their inquiries. Turns out she was acting strangely because she had a bee trapped in her hair. Apparently, she had a beehive hairdo, and the bee got confused."

Brian shrugged. "Do bees get confused? I thought bees were supposed to be intelligent."

"Did you ever hear of a bee performing brain surgery?"

"Well, no, but—"

"—Ever hear of a bee flying a plane?"

Brian thought for a moment. "Well, no, but—"

"So, how can you say that bees are intelligent?"

"Compared to other creatures, bees are intelligent."

"Like what other creatures?"

"Bees are more intelligent than evangelical Christians."

"Well, that's true. But a bowl of custard is more intelligent than an evangelical Christian. A nasty unexplained stain on your underwear is more intelligent than an evangelical Christian."

"Ok, I agree. Bees are not the brightest creatures." Brian poured a glass of orange juice. "So now they think Donna Reed's pubic wig was stolen by a man dressed up as a woman. It's puzzling. Whatever the gender of the thief, how do they know it's the same person? They must know something we don't. And what was Jed, our ice cream guy, doing visiting the Donna Reed Fan Club? That was too much of a coincidence. Why was he so interested in her hairbrush? Then his grandmother's Donna Reed memorabilia goes missing. These are questions that need to be answered. Listen—shh! The workmen are back next door. It's time for our crack of dawn breakfast."

Stéphane got to the glory hole first. He pulled back the latch and peered through the hole.

"Can you see anything?"

"Oh yes, more butt crack. Lots of it."

Brian pushed Stéphane aside. "That one with the shaved head and the tattoo of a rock 'n' roll Jesus on his back. I can feel myself being drawn into the inner Narnia between his butt cheeks. You don't have to go through a wardrobe—there are many ways into Narnia. Not many people know there's a secret world beyond a man's sphincter. A fantastic world hidden inside that pink puckered carnation of love ... that chocolate starfish ... that rusty bullet hole, that winking eye that calls out to complete strangers in the street, 'Hello Sailor.'"

"You're becoming quite poetic, Brian." Stéphane pushed Brian aside. "Oh my god, that tall one. Delicious!"

"But what are they actually doing over there?"

Stéphane shrugged. "No idea, but the whole garden is now gravel, and they're moving in strategically placed rocks."

"No sign of the new neighbors then?"

"No. I guess we'll meet them at some point." Stéphane closed the glory hole.

Brian spread marmalade on a slice of toast. "I know we were supposed to be doing something today, but I've forgotten what it was. Old age. Memory is going."

"We're going to the La Quinta Art Fair. We're looking for something to cover that bare wall in the lounge. Since you shot my idea down, about painting a mural myself."

"Stéphane, that's because you can't paint.'

"I think I know more about art than you do. You're a philistine. You don't know anything about art. For example, you said you didn't like Van Gogh's 'Starry Night' because you thought it was blurred."

"It is blurred."

"And you said that Picasso couldn't paint eyes because he painted them on the same side of a person's head."

"Well, he did."

"You also said the Pre-Raphaelites were a bunch of fucked-up twots— I believe that was the phrase you used."

"Well, they were."

"And I remember you telling all and sundry when we saw 'The Day Dream' by Dante Gabriel Rossetti at the Victoria and Albert Museum in London—"

"—Don't bring up the London trip."

"We were escorted out of the building."

"It's not my fault that some people can't take criticism."

"Brian, you tried to take the painting off the wall. They thought you were stealing it. We spent the whole week in jail. If it wasn't for that guy at the American Embassy, we'd still be there. They escorted us to Heathrow airport and put us on a plane. They couldn't wait to see the back of us."

"He had gorgeous blue eyes."

"Who had gorgeous blue eyes?"

"That nice man from the American Embassy."

Stéphane bit his lip and stared at his shoes.

Downtown La Quinta is a pretty area of coffee shops, boutiques, and stores selling essential oils, i.e., oils that aren't in the slightest bit essential. In fact, nothing on sale in downtown La Quinta is essential. It's all fripperies, as Maggie Smith would say in *Downton Abbey*. On the La Quinta Art Fair weekend, the main street was closed off to traffic, and every artist from miles around had a booth there. Brian and Stéphane wandered from booth to booth, perusing the artwork. One artist specialized in metalwork. Brian was impressed by his six-foot-tall dragons breathing fire. After half an hour, the tsunami of abstract art began to tear at their eyeballs, so they sat outside Le Roi Grenouille, a French patisserie. Brian and Stéphane watched the crowds trail back and forth. Brian ordered a banana and chocolate crepe, and iced tea. Brian, a slice of quiche and green salad.

Three elegantly dressed women at the next table talked loudly through botoxed lips. They looked like fat-lipped Muppets after an ugly brawl outside an upscale nail salon. "Did you read the paper this morning? Frontpage. Do we really have to have news about [whispers] pubic wigs?" The woman's face was in its early sixties, but her neck was eighty. She clung to her fading beauty like a man overboard clinging to a raft.

"I know. I saw it too. I immediately phoned the editor. I called on behalf of the La Quinta Ladies for Moral Decency. I told him, 'We're not going to put up with all this filth.'"

Stéphane and Brian were rapt.

A third woman, who looked like she'd been starched, opened her purse. "I picked this up at one of these booths. It says this person does personal nude photography. That's porn. Why do they assume that we want other people's genitals rammed down our throat willy nilly? I'm sick and tired of turning on the television and seeing naked people and hearing filthy language. And those animal shows aren't any better. Do we really need to see two orangutans copulating in a jungle. I walked in on my grandchildren the other day and found them watching the sex life of stick insects on TV. I almost vomited. I switched it off. And back to Donna Reed, I don't believe she wore such a thing. Hair extensions are for the head, not *down there*. The whole thing is ridiculous—fake news."

The first woman tried to sip her iced tea, but it dribbled from her fat lips onto her chin. She dabbed at it with a napkin. "I need a straw. I can't believe they put an object like a personal wig into an exhibition. I never even knew such a thing existed. What would be the purpose of it? It doesn't add to the memory of Donna Reed. In fact, it sullies it. I can never see a picture of Donna Reed now without thinking of her 'down there' area."

Brian lazily pushed the remnants of his quiche around the plate with his fork. Stéphane stared off into space.

The first woman straightened her emerald brooch. "And then one of the artists here is openly homosexual. Nothing against them, of course. One of them does my hair. But do they have to flaunt it? You don't see me parading around the streets dressed as the Village People."

"That's because you're a boring asshole." Brian smiled sweetly and ate the last piece of quiche on his plate. "But I do like your scarf. Gorgeous!"

The color drained from the woman's face.

"But—and it pains me to point this out—that tacky green brooch doesn't go with that pink K Mart dress. I'm a homosexual, so I know about these things. Sucking cock and picking out a fabulous outfit—that's where we shine. We've got nothing better to do with our lives than make straight people look pretty. And that's because God knows you have no idea how to present yourself to the world. My advice is to look in a mirror before you leave the house. La Quinta is so pretty. They don't need you three making the place look ugly. Have you considered wearing a bag over your head? So maybe a light blue dress might be more suitable. Most assholes can wear blue, can't they, Stéphane?"

"Yes, they can. Especially *complete* assholes. And you, madam, are a complete asshole. Now orange is a different story. Assholes can't wear orange, nor can dickheads."

"That's true, Stéphane. Assholes look terrible in orange. So do fuckbrains. Of course, titwads can wear anything. But none of you are titwads. And—this is only a suggestion—but perhaps fewer donuts in your diet. Next time you see a Krispy Kreme 'Hot Now' sign, keep driving. Fight the urge to gorge on a dozen chocolate iced custard-filled yummies in the parking lot."

"I agree, Brian. It's impossible to look stylish when you're carrying that much tonnage." Stéphane gesticulated grandly, knocking the first women's purse onto the ground. He picked it up and handed it back to her. "I'm sorry. Oh, it's a Valentino Garavani. A knockoff, of course. Who can afford the real thing? Not you, that's for sure. Did you buy it from that market stall in Indio? I think her name is Buffy—she makes these bags in a shed in her backyard."

The La Quinta Ladies for Moral Decency froze like statues; a Mount Rushmore of face-lifted interfering hags with tight trampoline faces and stiff perms. Perms so stiff, they could headbutt a rhino senseless.

Brian paid the bill. "Well, it was nice talking to you, you selfish assholes. I want to thank you because however bad I think I'm behaving in the future, I'll never be a bigger asshole than you three are right now. It was lovely meeting you, and I hope you all die horribly in a plane crash."

As they walked away, Stéphane smiled. "That was nicely handled."

"It was either that or I dropped my pants, stuck a kazoo up my ass and farted Tchaikovsky's 1812 Overture at them."

"Calling them assholes was a much better choice. I've heard your Tchaikovsky's 1812 Overture, and it's not all it's cracked up to be. But your 'German Requiem' by Brahms is a triumph."

Some of the vendors were packing up their booths at the Art Fair. One dark-haired woman, muscular, with Z cup breasts, loaded paintings onto a truck.

Stéphane stopped in his tracks. "Brian, look at that."

"What am I looking at? The boobs! I think they're probably in the Guinness Book of Records. They're huge."

"I'm talking about the painting, not the boobs. Although, the boobs are impressive. No, that painting over there. The colors go with our sofa in the living room. We can hang the picture behind it on the wall. Black and blue, it's perfect."

"I see you're looking at my painting. It's called Mute. I'm the artist. My name's Marjorie Titterson. I call it Mute because the subject matter is silent and cannot speak."

"What do you think, Brian?"

Brian glanced at the price label. "It's perfect. We'll take it."

Marjorie wrapped the painting. As she did so, she keeled over and fell on her face in the grass. Brian panicked. "What happened?"

"I think she's dead. Brian—look." Stéphane pointed.

"Oh no, one of her tits has fallen out. No bra! She's got the biggest tits on the planet, and one of them has fallen out, and she's dead, and she's not wearing a bra. This only ever happens to us. If we're sitting on a bus and one person on board has their mother's head in a jar at home, that person will sit down next to us and tell us all about it. If there's anyone around that has an erotic interest in camels, they will come up and tell us about it. There's something wrong with us. We're nut magnets. Now we're buying a painting from a dead woman with her tit hanging out."

"Put it back in her sweater."

"What?"

"Her tit. Put her tit back into her sweater. She deserves some kind of dignity."

"Stéphane, I'm not putting her tit back into her sweater. Oh damn! Now the other one has flopped out. They look like jellyfish washed up on a lonely beach."

"Give the woman some dignity. No woman wants to be found dead with her tits hanging out. Maybe Melania Trump, but aside from her. Ask any woman how she wants to die. Not one of them would say, 'I want to die at an Art Fair with my tits hanging out."

"Well, why don't *you* do it?"

"I can't touch a woman's breast. I'm gay."

"So am I."

"Yes, Brian, but I'm *really* gay. *Really, really, really* gay."

Just then, Marjorie Titterson began to stir.

Brian breathed a sigh of relief. "Thank goodness. Are you alright?"

Marjorie nodded and folded her breasts back into her V-neck sweater. "I'm sorry, I suffer from narcolepsy. I just pass out. Let me wrap this painting for you."

As Brian and Stéphane were leaving the Art Fair with their painting, they were stopped by two cops. The three women from the French patisserie were with them.

"That's them." One of the women pointed. "They shouted at us in a threatening manner. We were violated. Filthy language."

Stéphane stepped forward. "We were shouting at you because we caught you picking a man's pocket. And we told you to give that man his wallet back. You refused."

The woman bristled. "I have no idea what you're talking about. Arrest these men."

"If you look in her purse, you'll find the man's wallet."

"This is outrageous!" The woman emptied her purse out onto a table outside a booth selling portraits of dead rock stars.

"There it is!" Stéphane pointed to a man's wallet. "Is that your wallet? I don't think so! We saw you stealing it. Didn't we, Brian?"

"Yes, we saw her and her friends here picking pockets."

One of the policemen picked up the wallet and opened it. "Are any of you three ladies called David Johnson?" The three women shook their heads. "Well, I think I'm going to have to take you three to the station."

The cop turned to Stéphane. "Can you give me a description of the man they stole this from?"

"Yes, he was an older man in a wheelchair. He was wearing one of those Vietnam Vet caps. He had one leg and was blind."

Brian sighed. "I think it's sad when these thugs steal from the disabled. Someone who served our country valiantly."

The cops cuffed the three women and led them away.

Stéphane and Brian watched until they were out of sight.

"Stéphane, I see you still keep that dummy wallet in your pocket in case you're mugged. The one with the phony credit cards, outdated club membership cards, and the old driver's license you found tucked away in that briefcase you bought at that thrift store in Monterey."

"Yes. I just planted the wallet in her purse."

"Nice job."

"Thank you. I knew they'd be trouble. That much Botox can addle the brain."

At home, they unloaded the painting and hung it on the wall behind the sofa. Stéphane stood back and folded his arms across his chest. "It's perfect, the black and the blue compliment the sofa. But what is it?"

"It's a bunch of blobs. I don't think it's supposed to be anything. They look a bit like little misshapen penises. Didn't she say it was called Mute, and the subject of the painting was silent and could not speak?"

"Yes, she said that, but you know what artists are like with their airy-fairy bullshit. The colors of the blobby penises go with the sofa. That's all you need to know."

The doorbell rang. Stéphane answered it to find Alice on the doorstep with a sleeping Mitzi in her arms. "Is Brian here?"

"Come in. Brian, Alice is here with Mitzi."

Brian stiffened. He hated that damn dog. "Hi, Alice! What's the matter with Mitzi?" Mitzi was comatose.

"She's on these new pills the vet gave her to calm her down. The other day she got the mailman in the ankles. She's such an angry little thing." Mitzi's tongue lolled out of her mouth, and a string of drool hung down like a pearl necklace.

Brian smiled. "Poor thing."

Mitzi could see Brian through her drugged-up haze. She hated him— She hated him with every bone in her body.

Alice sank into the sofa. "I'm here to find out if you're going to Garth's talk at the community center."

Brian shuddered. Garth's only topic of conversation was humping Vietnamese whores and solving problems. "What's the talk about?"

"It's called 'Living with Herpes.' You know, the Greek God Herpes. Wait a minute, this painting. Is that new? It's by Marjorie Titterson."

"Do you know her?" Brian was surprised.

"Of course, I was on a carpentry course with her. We made birdcages together. But there's one thing—I hope you don't mind me saying this— but you've got the painting upside down. It's supposed to be the other way up. It's one of her Mute series, isn't it?"

"Yes, she said the subject is silent. It cannot speak. But we don't know what that means."

Alice smiled. "That's true. It can't speak."

Brian removed the painting, turned it around, and hung it up again.

Alice examined the painting closely. "You see, the painting is of a cascading waterfall of black and blue vaginas. Mute, the labia are lips that are silent and cannot speak. They have been beaten black and blue by male supremacy. Kicked between the legs. Oh yes, I remember Marjorie, alright. She's living proof that you can be a strong and powerful feminist and still have a great pair of tits."

At the sight of cascading bruised vaginas, Brian's jaw dropped. Stéphane passed out cold.

15

The Drag Show

The parking lot outside the White Swallow was packed. Stéphane and Brian hadn't been to a bar since they arrived in Palm Springs. The last drag show they saw was in Chicago at Meldrew's, an old former speakeasy on Mannheim Road in the suburbs.

"Stéphane, I hope this drag show is better than the last one we went to."

"I remember it well. The organizers said Dolly Parton slapping Diana Ross was intentional, a part of the show. It was staged. I believe that."

"And what about the wig-pulling? When they put the winning tiara on Tina Turner, and Jennifer Lopez tore her wig off and punched her in the face—you think that was all part of the show?"

"Yes, I do."

"And what about the ugly brawl between Tammy Wynette and Joan Crawford that was staged, wasn't it? Even though Tammy was bleeding from a head wound."

"Yes, it was."

"And what about Cher pissing all over my shoes at the urinal. Was that part of the show?"

"That I don't know."

"And what about Patti LuPone sucking Amy Winehouse's dick in the men's room. Was that all part of the show? Because I saw that with my very own eyes. And I never want to see anything like that again. Call me old-fashioned, but I don't think drag queens should perform oral sex on each other in toilets. They should only perform oral sex on each other away from prying eyes, like in a bank vault or a coal mine."

Brian sighed. "I'd love to see coal miners in drag having sex with each other."

Brian and Stéphane were at the White Swallow to see Martie from the garden center. Who doesn't want to see a 350lb man pretending to be Peggy Lee? As they opened the door to the bar, the music poured out onto the street like slime from a slimeball. Neither Brian nor Stéphane, were fans of modern gay dance music. However, the place was hopping. Perhaps "hopping" isn't the right word for 200 male senior citizens on painkillers and blood thinners. You could almost smell the alpha-blockers. There was also a smattering of young men and a sprinkling of women. The dancefloor was packed with gyrating rheumatoid figures dancing under pulsating lights bouncing off the smallest disco ball in the world. It resembled an electrocuted testicle. Stéphane and Brian ordered Bacardi and Cokes and found a quiet spot where they could see the stage.

Stéphane caved in first. "I don't know how long I can stand up here. All the seats are taken."

Brian approached a table and whispered in a young man's ear. He talked to his friends, and they got up and relocated to the bar, giving Stéphane and Brian a table to sit at.

"Brian, how did you manage that?"

"I told them it was your birthday today, and you only had one week to live, and you wanted to see the drag show one more time. They were happy to give up their seats."

"What?"

"Just sit there, look sickly and on the brink of death. Gasp for air every so often."

"What am I supposed to be dying of?"

"I told them it was untreated syphilis."

Stéphane's jaw dropped. For once, he was speechless.

"Good evening bitches." The MC for the night, Columbia Cartel, climbed the four steps to the stage. She was dressed as a rather plump Patsy Cline. She tapped the microphone. "Is this fucking thing working? I apologize—Philip, can you get this thing working? Wait a minute—there we are. Good evening bitches! Welcome to the White Swallow. Tonight, we have a plethora—a plethora—try saying that with a mouthful of cock—a plethora of talent."

"Get on with it!" A voice in the audience shouted.

"Who said that?" Columbia Cartel rested her hand on her hip. She shielded her eyes with the other hand and scanned the audience. "Oh, there she is. I thought it was you. Honey, you should be down at the Ranch, they're having a Miss Tiny Meat contest. You're a shoo-in to win that. Didn't you win the Miss Toothpick contest last week? Anyway, do we have any virgins in the house tonight? A few hands. Where are you from, darlings?"

A timid voice answered. "Ontario."

"Ontario. We love snowbirds here at the White Swallow. Canada, the country that gave us ... ugh ... can't think of anything offhand. So let's give a big round of applause to our Canadian cousins." The crowd whooped and hollered. "Now, we've got a great show for you tonight, but before we start. We have a very special person in our audience. He's having some health issues now, but today is his birthday. So, let's sing Happy Birthday for Stéphane."

Stéphane and Brian turned beet red as the crowd sang "Happy Birthday."

Columbia Cartel continued. "I'm not going to ask how old you are. A lady never divulges her age. I'm guessing you're old enough to remember *The Donna Reed Show*. But some of you young'uns don't remember who Donna Reed was, do you? She was a TV star who always vacuumed, wearing heels and pearls. As do I. Have you been reading about that? I bet it was one of you bitches who stole her merkin. I'd wear it. Anyhow, let's move on. We've been doing our Parade of Stars show now for five years, and tonight is the best show yet. If you're politically correct, then get the fuck out. The show tonight will offend anyone who doesn't have a sense of humor. We don't put up with that PC nonsense here at the White Swallow." The crowd roared. "First up is Miss Nose Candy Darling."

Nose Candy Darling appeared from behind a curtain dressed as Carmen Miranda. "*Yi, Yi, Yi, Yi, I like you very much. I, Yi, Yi, Yi, Yi, I think you're grand. Why, why, why is it that when I feel your touch.*" As she lip-synched, she pulled an apple from her headpiece and ate it, tossing the core into the audience, followed by a pear.

The applause was deafening. The walls of the White Swallow shook. Columbia Cartel returned to the stage. "Well, wasn't that special? A fruit-eating fruit. Who doesn't like Carmen Miranda? Did you know she was Portuguese? And her real name was Maria do Carmo Miranda da Cunha. See bitches, I'm not just a pretty face." The audience laughed. "What are you bitches laughing at? Fuck you. Next up is Amber Alert."

Amber Alert was dressed as Baby Jane Hudson sucking on a lollipop. "*I've written a letter to Daddy. His address is Heaven above. I've written 'Dear Daddy, we miss you. And wish you were with us to love.'*" There were a few jeers in the crowd. Amber Alert bristled. "It's a fucking joke. Get over it."

Columbia Cartel returned to the stage. "If you thought that was bad taste, the next performer is Anna Rexia-Nervosa doing "We've Only Just Begun.""

Brian nudged Stéphane. "Can you get a couple more drinks? Your turn to push through the crowd."

Stéphane wilted. "I can't. I'm supposed to be dying next week. I'm riddled with syphilis, remember?"

"And the next performer is Martie Navratihomo doing Peggy Lee. Martie saw Stéphane and Brian in the crowd and waved. Then Peggy Lee snapped her fingers. "*Never know how much I love you. Never know how much I care When you put your arms around me. I get a fever that's so hard to bear. You give me fever when you kiss me, fever when you hold me tight. Fever, in the mornin', a fever all through the night—*"

There was a loud crash as the stage gave way, and Martie Navratihomo collapsed into a heap. Anna Rexia-Nervosa ran to Martie's aid. "Are you ok, darling? I know you've performed on a few shaky erections over the years, but this one tops it all."

"Let me through. I'm a doctor." Columbia Cartel pushed through the crowd.

Brian gasped. "She's a doctor!"

A man sitting next to Brian leaned across. "Columbia Cartel is a heart surgeon at Desert Regional Hospital. She's dating a Catholic priest. The priest is Nose Candy Darling. Never judge by appearances."

An ambulance arrived, and Martie was loaded onto a stretcher and taken away.

As Brian and Stéphane were leaving, a group of men was entering. One of them was Jimmie from the Donna Reed Fan Club. "Hey, you two, I didn't know you frequented the White Swallow, a true den of iniquity."

"You've just missed quite a show." Brian laughed. "Martie Navratihomo was carted off to hospital after the stage collapsed."

"Not again. One day this bar will get sued. Last year Raven Ann-Ranting skidded on a used condom in the bathroom and hit her head on the sink. What a shemozzle. Knocked the gay right out of her. Turned to Jesus after that. One minute she's turning tricks, next minute she's turning the pages of Leviticus and warning against the perils of homosexuality. Now she's a pastor at an evangelical church in Tucson. Speaking in tongues, the works. Amazing! That girl's had more dicks than you'd see at a convention of Richards."

16

The Moroccan Pot

At the breakfast table the following morning, Stéphane opened the *Desert Sun*. "There's more news about the Donna Reed pubic wig snatcher. Apparently, he's robbed another bank. Chase Bank in Indio. There's a picture." Stéphane held up the blurred picture of a hooded masked figure wearing sunglasses.

Brian studied the image. "That could be anybody."

"Well, not anybody, Brian."

"Yes, anybody. You look at the picture, and I'll say a name. You tell me if the person I name could be the person in the picture. Think about it carefully."

"Ok."

"Sean Connery."

Stéphane looked at the picture. "Well, yes, it could be Sean Connery."

"Goldie Hawn."

Stéphane looked at the picture again. "I see what you mean. Yes, these pictures are not very helpful. The figure is so covered up that it could be Goldie Hawn."

Brian twirled and waxed his non-existent mustache. "Howevair, eef I put on my Hercule Poiraht haht ahnd use my leettle gray cells, I nahtice sahmetheeng odd een ziss phahtograhph."

"What?"

"How hot was it yesterday?"

"It was 120 degrees. Hottest day of the year so far."

"Then why is the bank robber wearing a long sleeve sweatshirt? And why are the sleeves taped to his wrists? Could it be that he's hiding a dragon tattoo on his arm?"

"It's possible. The police might be right. The wig snatcher and the bank robber are the same person. And it could be Jed, our ice cream seller. The problem is that it could also be Goldie Hawn. Though it's unlikely. Why would Goldie Hawn be robbing a bank in Indio? Shoplifting—maybe. Picking pockets—I can see her doing that."

"Really, Stéphane? I don't see Goldie Hawn as a shoplifter or pickpocket. Now, I can see Julie Andrews robbing a bank."

"Definitely. She's shady. I never fell for that *Mary Poppins* goody-two-shoes image. There's something psychotic about Julie Andrews. She could have been Hannibal Lector in *Silence of the Lambs*."

"You know who else it could be—Barry Manilow."

"Fuck you, Brian. We agreed we would never again mention the name of Barry Manilow."

"Sshhh! Voices next door."

Stéphane made it to the glory hole first. "I think our new neighbors have arrived."

Brian pushed Stéphane aside. "Wait a minute, I recognize him. But I can't remember where I've seen him before. Oh, wait a minute. He's the guy—oh damn!"

"What's wrong?"

"It's the guy from the supermarket. I can't remember his name, something stupid like Horace Beaverbutt—no, that's not it. Harry Larktree—no, that's not it either. Potter Hogwart? It was the day you saw the tarantula and all hell broke loose. He was recommending a strawberry yogurt to me. He said he was moving to Palm Springs with his wife to open a meditation school. I seem to remember that he got arrested for shoplifting in all the chaos. He probably blames us. That's going to be awkward. What's that noise? I think I can hear a truck out front."

Stéphane ran to the front of the house, to the mailbox. Then returned. "Yep, that's a moving van. They're moving in today. I picked up the mail." Stéphane opened the first letter. "Gas bill, another 20% off coupon at Bed, Bath, and Beyond—oh, what's this? This was hand-delivered. It's an invitation to meet our new neighbors and their family. Apparently, it's a house cleansing, whatever that is. Fiorella, a Peruvian priestess, will be in attendance to exorcise any racism or homophobia that may have been left by the previous owner."

Brian bristled. "Graham wasn't racist or homophobic. That's a bit of an assumption, isn't it?"

"I guess they're just hedging their bets. Their name is Riverlight."

"That's it! That's the name of the guy in the supermarket, Erik Riverlight, and his wife's name was—I forget."

"Heather. Heather and Erik Riverlight."

"Now I understand what was happening in the garden. He said he was building a Zen Garden. That's why all the plants were removed. When is this house cleansing?"

"Tomorrow at 4 pm. Should we buy the Riverlights a housewarming gift? Why don't we buy a gift at the Antiques Fair on Sunny Dunes? It's today. What would a couple like that want?"

"Stéphane, people like that would be happy with a piece of tree bark and a couple of acorns. New age, spiritual, free thinkers, bohemians, beatniks—whatever you call them these days, they're basically hippies."

Sunny Dunes in Palm Springs is the antique store area, and once a month, they host an Antiques Street Fair. Brian and Stéphane were regular attendees—Stéphane collected compacts and powder puffs, and Brian, Carolyn Keene's Nancy Drew Mystery books and vintage salt and pepper shakers. In their house in Twilight Manors, there were two glass cabinets for prize items in their collections, one for Stéphane and one for Brian. They were also avid *Antiques Roadshow* fans. They even had their favorite appraisers. Brian liked Nicholas Lowry, the man with the outrageous suits who appraised posters. Stéphane liked Noel Barrett, the ponytailed appraiser of vintage toys. They longed for the *Antiques Roadshow* to return to Palm Springs. They wanted to appear in the Feedback Booth and say, in unison, "We thought our antique Chinese dildo from the Wang period was priceless, but it turns out to be something they made for tourists in the 1930s."

It was mid-afternoon when they arrived at the Sunny Dunes Antiques Fair. It opened at midday, and most of the early-bird crowd had come and gone. Brian was branching out into the Power Boys Series of books by Mel Lyle—they were cheap and turned up in thrift stores all the time. Brian had no interest in collecting items of value. He collected for the joy of collecting. Stéphane, on the other hand, *was* interested in value. His collection of powder puffs and compacts was worth several thousand dollars. He had three 1930s mirrored compacts made by Ripley & Gowan, valued at $400 each. He had 375 items in his collection. That's how he earned his platinum Gay Card. That and hanging around truck stops in his youth wearing a miniskirt and a halter top.

Brian bought two Power Boys books at the first booth, *The Mystery of the Haunted Skyscraper* and *The Mystery of the Double Kidnapping*. He hoped one day to find copies of the extremely rare, *The Mystery of the Double-Headed Appliance* and *The Mystery of the Breeding Ass*.

At the second booth, Brian found a Moroccan pot. "This might be a nice gift for the neighbors' house cleansing party."

"It's pretty, but is it hippy-dippy enough for them? Shouldn't it be blessed by a shaman or something? Is there any way we can rub it up against a Tibetan monk? Or get it fingered by the Pope?"

"Fingered by the Pope? It's a pot, not a choirboy."

"I might be able to help with that."

The man was in his fifties, handsome, with a cowboy hat and a long straggly salt and pepper beard. He wore a sleeveless check shirt, and his hair hung almost to his waist. "I'll bless it for you. I'll even write a note and put it inside the pot."

Brian laughed. "Are you a shaman, the Pope? I mean, these people are having a house cleansing with a Peruvian priestess, they have a Zen Garden, their name is Riverlight—you know the type. Spiritual, airy-fairy, nonsense types. Palm tree huggers. Granola and feng shui up to the eyeballs. Like you, actually—a bit of a hippie, like you."

The man laughed. "No, I'm not a shaman or a Pope, but I'm something even better. Something that will really impress them. I was a roadie for Grateful Dead and Jerry Garcia's tarot reader. I have a very hippy-dippy resume. I've had sex with two of Country Joe and the Fish. Mama Cass licked my balls in Laurel Canyon once. Need I go on?"

Stéphane sniggered. "Why stop now."

"I once had a threesome with Janis Joplin and a bottle of fabric softener."

Brian opened his wallet. The booth owner scribbled on a piece of paper. "This Moroccan pot has been blessed by Johnny Cloudstar, a roadie for the Grateful Dead." Then he dropped the note into the pot and taped the lid shut.

Brian and Stéphane thanked Johnny Cloudstar and moved on to the next booth. While Brian bought *The Mystery of the Flying Skeleton* and *The Mystery of the Burning Ocean*, Stéphane aimlessly flicked through a box of movie stills. "Brian, look at this." It was a still of Donna Reed playing Molly Ford in *Shadow of the Thin Man,* and it was signed. "I'm going to buy it. We can add this to our own collection of Donna Reed memorabilia. We've already got *The Donna Reed Show Pictorial Memoir* that we bought in Yucca Valley. It's a bargain, though I'm guessing this autograph is fake." Stéphane paid the $20. "What do you think, Brian, real signature or fake?"

Stéphane thought it was Brian standing next to him, but when he turned, he found himself staring into the eyes of Jed, the ice-cream seller. "Hi, I recognize you from the Cold Comfort Shake Rattle and Roll Ice Cream Parlor. You get the Key Lime Pistachio cone, and your friend gets the Almond Joy shake. You're one of our regular customers. You probably don't recognize me. I work there. I'm Jed. I see you're a fan of Donna Reed."

"Yes, I am. Are you?" Stéphane smiled.

"No, not me. That was a bit before my time. But my grandmother worked for Donna Reed. She had a few items in her memorabilia collection, but she was recently burgled, and it was all stolen. So I'm trying to buy some Donna Reed items to cheer her up. Would you consider selling me that picture? You got here before me. I'll give you $50 for it. The autograph is a fake, by the way."

Brian appeared. "No, sorry, it's not for sale."

"What about $100? That's my final offer."

"No, this is going into our collection. We have a large collection of Donna Reed memorabilia, don't we, Stéphane?"

"Yes, we do. We've got one of her hats. Not one that she wore in a movie or on TV, but one of her personal hats. One of my uncles was her gardener. Donna Reed gave the hat to him for his wife, as she admired it. After my aunt passed away, he donated it to my collection. I also have a pair of her shoes and a bra."

Jed's eyes flashed with excitement. "Would you consider selling me the hat, shoes, and bra?"

Brian stood firm. "No, we're keeping them."

"I'll pay you $1,000 for them."

"I'm sorry, they're not for sale."

"Well, let me know if you change your mind. You know where to find me."

When Stéphane and Brian left the Antiques Fair, they noticed Jed watching them. Brian warned. "He's going to follow us. He wants to know where we live. Mark my words. Don't walk toward the car. Walk in the opposite direction." Brian and Stéphane walked along Palm Canyon Drive, then turned a corner and hightailed it back to the car. Brian jumped into the driver's seat. "Let's get the hell out of here. That was creepy."

As they drove home, Brian noticed a car following them. "Let's take a different route. This must be Jed, trying to find out where we live." Every turn they took, the car followed them. They turned onto Ramone Avenue and headed away from Palm Springs through Cathedral City, then to Palm Desert and beyond. It was early evening now, and the sun was low in the sky. Soon they were in the open desert and still being followed. Brian turned off and drove up a smaller road, past a cactus farm and the Sidewinder Saloon. The car followed them. Suddenly the car behind them speeded up and tried to overtake them. Brian accelerated. The car tried to overtake them again, but Brian swerved into it this time. The other vehicle careened off the road and into a shallow ditch. Brian drove on.

Stéphane's heart pounded. "Who was that?"

"I'm not stopping and getting out of the car to find out." Brian headed home.

Safely back in Twilight Manors, Brian sank into a sofa. "I can't believe someone tried to run us off the road. They were after that photograph we bought."

"I don't think it was Jed. His story about replacing his grandmother's stolen Donna Reed items sounds believable to me. It fits in with the story his grandmother, Angelica Fosgrave, told us. I think someone else followed us, and for another reason entirely, but who and why?"

"Where would someone who lives in an RV and works in an ice cream parlor get $1000? But you might be right. Perhaps we're misreading the signs. Who would try to run us off the road? And why? And don't say it was Goldie Hawn."

"I wasn't going to say Goldie Hawn. I was thinking it might have been Barry Manilow."

"Fuck you, Stéphane. We agreed to never mention that man's name. I can't stand him. I've never liked him. His music is crap. Now, you've got me started."

"I don't like him either."

"Then stop mentioning his name."

17
The House Cleansing

Brian rang the doorbell. It was answered by Erik Riverlight and his beaming teeth. It looked like he had a mouthful of lightbulbs. "Welcome to our new home."

"In case you don't know, we live next door. I'm Brian and this is Stéphane, my husband. Thank you for the invitation."

"Please come in. We're outside in the garden." Erik led the way through a sparsely furnished house. "We're minimalists. A strategically placed feather here, a pinecone there. One of our daughters is a feng shui master. This is really her creation. Excuse me." Erik picked up a copy of *Bhagavad Gita* on a coffee table and moved it three inches to the right. He produced a tape measure from his back pocket and checked it was placed correctly. "Are you familiar with feng shui?"

"Not really, no." Brian shook his head.

"I read an article once in *Vanity Fair*, but I never fully understood what it was about." Stéphane had zero interest in feng shui.

"Feng shui is a method of balancing yin and yang and improving the flow of chi by arranging furniture."

Brian smiled. "And what exactly is chi?"

Flustered, Erik changed the subject. "Let me take you through to the garden."

Brian whispered to Stéphane. "As I suspected, no idea what he's talking about. I think he's forgotten ever meeting me. Either that or he's decided our meeting is not to be mentioned. How tactful of him. We'll just let the supermarket incident drop."

There were about fifty guests in the Zen Garden, including some of the residents of Twilight Manors. Jeffrey Collier was there—he had a nervous breakdown when Wham! split up and never fully recovered. Actors Alice, Jennie, and their sedated chihuahua, Mitzi were there. Also, Bimbo and Betsy were there—a sturdy couple who claimed not to be lesbians but lived together and wore men's shoes. Enthusiastic golf players. Gold star members of the Melissa Etheridge fan club, they met on an Olivia Cruise back in 1990. But they're not lesbians.

"Heather!" Erik called out to a cluster of people on the far side of the pool. "Come and meet our next-door neighbors, Stéphane and Brian."

Heather was a pretty woman in her early fifties. She wore a smock and a long, flowered skirt. Her hair was piled up on her head like a tangled bird's nest. She was one of those people who wouldn't mind if birds nested in her hair. In fact, she'd love it. Heather placed her fingertips together and bowed. "Tashi deleg. That's a Tibetan greeting."

Brian, struggling to keep a straight face, gave her the gift.

"Oh, it's beautiful. Moroccan, I believe. In that case I must say mrehba—but whatever the language, welcome to our home."

"There's a message inside the pot."

Heather opened the pot and read the message from Johnny Cloudstar. "Oh, my goodness, it's been blessed by a roadie for the Grateful Dead. How wonderful. We used to follow Grateful Dead around the country selling candles and jewelry, didn't we Erik?"

"Yes, those were good times. Before we settled down and you became a dream therapist and I studied massage therapy and transcendental meditation. Everyone should wander a while before they settle in one place. We were gypsies in our youth."

"You're a dream therapist!" Suddenly Stéphane was interested. "I have this recurring dream of being chased by a giant rabbit wearing a leather bustier and crocs."

"It sounds like you have unresolved issues with your mother. But I'm not talking shop today. Instead, I'd like to introduce you to our family." She beckoned several young people, then gathered them together like a mother hen with her chicks. "These are my daughters, Anise, Cinnamon, and Saffron. Turmeric couldn't be here, as she's travelling in India. Nor could Sumac, she's a scientologist, so we don't see much of her these days. Lives in a compound in New Mexico. We send her food parcels, but I don't think she gets them. We also have two sons. This is Ginger and Caraway. As you can see, Caraway is a Benedictine monk. He's attending a retreat in the high desert and managed to slip away. Ginger is an Elvis impersonator."

Brian whispered to Stéphane. "This isn't a family, this is a spice rack."

"I'd also like you to meet my grandchildren. These are Cinnamon's children, Elderberry, Gooseberry, Raspberry, and Dingleberry—they were all adopted from Cambodia. Cinnamon's husband, Leaf, is studying under the Maharisha Mahesh Yogurt in the Hindu Kush, so he can't be here. Last time we saw him, he was wearing saffron robes and odd socks."

Brian focused on a hummingbird hovering nearby. Stéphane smiled like a halfwit and zoned out.

Heather continued. "And this is Saffron's husband, Ocean, and their children, Turnip, Cauliflower, and Carrot. And these are Anise's two sons, Basil, and Parsley. I'm afraid Anise's husband, Wind Flame, passed away recently, when a herb rack fell onto his head. He fell over and landed on a bread knife. Very sad. My other children have chosen celibacy, but that could change at any moment. I wouldn't rule out the pattering of more tiny feet, a little Eggplant, Sweetcorn, or Parsnip, at some future date. We also have three cats, Jasper, Amethyst, and Turquoise: Jasper is the reincarnation of Cleopatra; Amethyst is the reincarnation of Catherine the Great; and Turquoise is the reincarnation of Betty Boop. They're all vegan. In fact, the whole family are vegan."

Brian reeled from the tsunami of silly, primarily plant-based names. "You have a wonderful family. Excuse me, I've just seen someone I know." Brian joined Alice, Jennie, and a sedated Mitzi. The Riverlight clan dispersed like a paintball splatting into a brick wall.

Stéphane spoke to Caraway. "I think you're the first Benedictine monk that I've met."

"Oh really, my dear. I'm sure you've bumped into lots of us in leather bars. But you must tell me, where did you buy that fabulous bracelet?"

Stéphane choked on the cloud of fairy dust flying off this monk. He took a step back to avoid being slapped in the face by Caraway's flamboyant gestures; he looked like a windmill having a stroke.

Caraway continued. "I used to have a bracelet like that, but Father Robert borrowed it for Halloween, and I never got it back. Bitch! But that's typical of her. She was never the same after she got her foreskin caught in a sailor's zip ... long story. I'll tell you about it sometime. Anyway, I do miss that bracelet. It complimented this angora sweater I bought in New York. Was it Macey's? It might have been Bloomingdales. I can't remember now. I do know where I lost it. I picked up this truck driver last year. Anyway, I left the sweater in his truck. It's probably somewhere in Idaho now. He probably gave it to his wife. There's some chain-smoking white trash woman wearing my angora sweater right now, as we speak. Oh well, c'est la vie. You're cute. Do you and your husband play around on each other?"

Stéphane was shocked. "No, we're married."

Caraway blanched. His face twisted with anger. "Not in the eyes of God you're not. You're an abomination." With that, the Benedictine monk turned and walked away in a huff.

"I see you've pissed off my brother."

Stéphane turned. It was Ginger. "Yes, I did. He seems confused about some things."

"Don't worry about him. He's just jealous that you and your husband are so open. He can't seem to escape his own darkness. That's why they become monks in the first place. But the truth is, you can't run away from yourself. That's like trying to outrun your shadow."

"Your mother said you're an Elvis impersonator."

"Yes, I'm the apple that fell a long way away from the family tree. I'm an actor. Currently I'm playing Elvis Presley in a one man show at the

Blue Room. I wrote it myself. The show is called *Priscilla Presley, Queen of the Desert*. It's the story of Elvis' last few days seen through the eyes of his wife, Priscilla. I compare his last few days to drag queens driving across the desert in the *Priscilla, Queen of the Desert* movie. I don't know if you know this, but Elvis and Priscilla honeymooned here in Palm Springs. You should come and see the show. Wait!" Ginger fumbled in his pocket. He handed Stéphane two complimentary tickets for the following Saturday. "For you and Brian."

"Thank you, we'll definitely be there. Excuse me, I must tell Brian."

Stéphane joined Brian, who was talking to Bimbo and Betsy. "Brian, we've got tickets to see Ginger in a show."

"Not a drag show, is it? Not after the other one. By the way, I found out this morning that Martie is recovering nicely."

"Who's Martie?" Bimbo thought she'd heard the name before.

"Martie owns a gardening center in Palm Desert and is also a drag queen. We saw him recently at the White Swallow and he was hurt when the stage collapsed."

"Oh dear. That happened to us once, back when we were a duet. I played piano and Betsy sang. We were halfway through 'I Am Woman,' the Helen Reddy song, when the stage collapsed under the weight of the piano. It was at the Michigan Women's Music Festival. But we're not lesbians. That's a common mistake people make about us, isn't it Betsy?"

"Yes, it is. People think that because we watch tennis on TV and build our own bookshelves, that we're lesbians, but we're not."

Heather Riverlight clapped her hands. "Can I get everyone's attention. I'd like to introduce you to Fiorella, a Peruvian priestess, who will now cleanse our new home."

Fiorella, wearing predictable flowing robes, lit a candle. "I have come from the mountains of Peru, acrawss rivahs and desahts, to be heeuh to bless this house." She then lit sage from a candle and began smudging. "Deah gawddess, I thank you faw this family, I pray that throughout this home Erik and Heathah Rivahlight will be able to feel youh presence. In the name of the gawddess, am'n."

Brian leaned into Stéphane, "What's with the Boston accent?"

"Haven't you heard? Boston is full of Peruvian priestesses. You can't walk ten feet without tripping over one. They're like cockroaches. I once read this article about a house in Boston that was infested with Peruvian priestesses. They tented it and pumped poison in, but the Peruvian priestesses wouldn't die. So, in the end, they had to burn the house down. Anyway, I need the bathroom—do you know where it is?"

In the bathroom, Stéphane lowered himself onto the toilet seat. To his right, he noticed a blue button. He pressed it and a jet of water shot up into his honey pot. Stéphane squealed.

In the garden again, Brian bristled. "You took your time. Don't leave me alone here with these nutjobs. I've just been talking to Anise, or it may have been Cinnamon. I don't know, it was one of the spice girls. Anyway, she was telling me about healing crystals."

"They've got a bidet." Stéphane blurted it out. "You have to try it."

"I've never used a bidet before. What's it like?"

"It's like getting your asshole licked by a dolphin."

"Really! I love dolphins. I used to watch *Flipper* when I was a kid. I can even remember the theme song. *They call him Flipper, Flipper, faster than lightning. No-one you see, is smarter than he, and we know Flipper, lives in a world full of wonder, flying there-under, under the sea*! Let me try this bidet. I'll report back."

Brian headed off to the bathroom. Ten minutes later, he returned. "I see what you mean. We must have one installed in our bathroom. I love dolphins. And, from what I've just experienced, dolphins love me."

"Have what installed?" Alice was standing next to them.

Brian whispered. "The Riverlights have a bidet."

"Oh really, I've never tried one before. Did you hear that, Jennie? The Riverlights have a bidet."

"I've never tried a bidet. What's it like?"

Brian panicked. "It's—it's refreshing."

"I have to try it." Alice disappeared with Mitzi in her arms. Twenty minutes later, she hadn't returned. Brian, Stéphane, and Jennie went to find her. Jennie knocked on the bathroom door. "Alice, are you alright in there?"

"It won't switch off. The bidet, it won't switch off. There's water gushing."

"Come and open the door."

"I can't. If I stand up the water will spray everywhere."

Brian stepped forward. "Alice put the lid down on the toilet. That'll stop it spraying over the whole room.

"I tried that, but it sprays out the side. There's water everywhere."

"Unlock the door fast and then sit down again. We can clear up the mess."

Alice stood up, opened the door, and then sat down again as fast as she could. Which, for a woman who appeared in the original stage production of *The King and I* in 1951, wasn't very fast at all. Water sprayed everywhere. "I'm soaked! And poor Mitzi is furious."

Stéphane, Brian, and Jennie crammed into the bathroom and locked the door behind them. A wet Alice was sitting on the toilet with a dripping Mitzi. "This is so embarrassing."

"Brian leaned over and pressed the blue button hard. "No, it's not working. You get off the toilet and let me sit there while I work out how to turn this thing off. Everybody grab a towel and start cleaning the place up."

Alice eased herself off the toilet, and Brian sat down in her place. "Oh no!" Brian buried his face in his hands. "I forgot to pull my jeans and underwear down. My jeans are getting soaked. My ass is soaked." Brian stabbed at the button. Finally, after twenty or so stabs, the water stopped. The floor and walls, sink and vanity, Alice, Jennie and Mitzi, Brian and Stéphane were all soaking wet.

There was a knock at the door—Stéphane opened it a couple of inches. The Riverlight clan was standing outside. Erik gently pushed the door open. "Everything ok in there? You're all soaking wet. Brian, look at the back of your jeans. What happened?"

Stéphane stepped forward. "I'm afraid Brian has had a mishap. Enlarged prostate, pressure on the urethra, prone to accidents. I do apologize. He's an old man. His piss factory is on the blink. You're probably wondering why there are two lesbians in the bathroom with us. Well, what can I say? Lesbians are always good in a crisis."

Erik pointed to Brian. "Now I know who you are. I knew I recognized you from somewhere. You're the guy in the supermarket."

18

Priscilla Presley, Queen of the Desert

There was quite a crowd at the Blue Room, Palm Springs' premiere dinner theater venue. Brian ordered a meatball pasta and Stéphane, shrimp scampi. It was a small, intimate venue, with only fifteen tables, each with starched white tablecloths and candles. The bare walls were hidden behind red velvet curtains. The owner, Pierre Beausoleil, was a flamboyant Frenchman whose English was patchy to say the least. Against all advice, he insisted on introducing the acts. "Welcome to the Blue Room and this night on which we stand here in these battered surroundings—we are plastered in exuberance by Ginger Riverlight's *Priscilla Presley, Queen of the Desert.* Many of yourselves will know that this is not Mr. Riverlight's first attendance at the Blue Room. He was present here a year earlier in *Jeffrey Dahmer: The Musical.* Please open your hearts to *Priscilla Presley, Plate of the Desserts.* No wait, I am being told something—what?—I'm being told that it was not *Jeffrey Dahmer: The Musical* but *Betty White: The Musical.* Not the same thing, they tell me. Who knew?"

The curtains opened. At the front of the stage were two giant circles that represented the eyes of Priscilla Presley. The audience was to look through them. They even had eyelashes. On the stage, props were minimal, just a microphone standing center stage and a shower curtain hanging up right stage.

Ginger made a convincing Fat Elvis—He wore a glittering padded rhinestone encrusted suit. Ginger was relatively slight. He took the microphone and sang "Viva Las Vegas" ... *"Bright light city gonna set my soul, gonna set my soul on fire. Got a whole lot of money that's ready to burn, so get those stakes up higher. There's a thousand pretty women waitin' out there. And they're all livin' the devil may care. And I'm just the devil with love to spare, so Viva Las Vegas, Viva Las Vegas."*

Ginger spoke of Elvis Presley's long journey across the desert of popular music. He likened the King's career to the epic journey of Mitzi, Felicia, and Bernadette in the movie *Priscilla, Queen of the Desert.* An hour later, Ginger pulled back the shower curtain to reveal a toilet.

Brian nudged Stéphane. "Another toilet. Haven't we had enough toilets?"

"Calm down, Brian, it can't be plumbed in. What can go wrong with a toilet that's not plumbed in?"

"Why is it there?"

"It's the last days of Elvis Presley. He died sitting on the toilet."

Brian gasped. "I never knew that."

"Lenny Bruce died on the toilet. A lot of famous people die on the toilet. Judy Garland."

"I didn't even know that Judy Garland *went* to the toilet, let alone died on one."

Ginger's Elvis Presley walked to the front of the stage and peeled off his fat suit. He stood on the stage completely naked.

Stéphane's eyes widened. "Well, I didn't see that coming."

"He's very impressive, isn't he?"

"He could throw that thing over his shoulder and burp it."

"If you think about it, nobody strips naked on stage if they've got a small dick, do they? It has to be big enough for the audience to see it. Unless you provide every member of the audience with a magnifying glass. Especially those in the cheap seats—They would need opera glasses at the very least."

Then Ginger's Elvis sang. *"I've been to Georgia and California and anywhere I could run. Took the hand of a preacher man. And we made love in the sun. But I ran out of places and friendly faces. Because I had to be free. I've been to paradise, but I've never been to me."*

"I didn't know Elvis sang that song."

"He didn't. That's from *Priscilla, Queen of the Desert.* He's making the connection between Elvis Presley and three Australian drag queens. A bit of a stretch if you ask me."

Then Ginger's Elvis bent over and showed the audience his rear end. He continued. "And then, on the night I died, I swallowed a handful of codeine." Ginger's Elvis slid ping pong balls into his rectum as he said this. The audience gasped. Seconds later, Ginger's Elvis fired the ping pong balls out of his ass and into the audience. One landed in the remnants of Stéphane's shrimp scampi. He grimaced and pushed the plate away.

The audience erupted into laughter while dodging ping pong balls. Then Ginger's Elvis sat on the toilet and quietly sang, "(There'll Be) Peace in the Valley" *"There will be peace in the valley for me, some day. There will be peace in the valley for me, oh Lord I pray. There'll be no sadness, no sorrow. No trouble, trouble I see. There will be peace in the valley for me, for me."* Ginger's Elvis leaned forward and toppled onto the floor when the song ended, firing off one last ping pong ball into the audience.

The lights dimmed, and the curtain closed.

As Brian and Stéphane were leaving, they bumped into Jimmie from the Donna Reed Fan Club. "You two again. Are you following me or am I following you?" He was with two friends, bearish men with pierced noses.

Brian laughed. "A bit of both."

"My friends and I are dropping into the Massive Rooster for a nightcap if you're interested in joining us. It's a wrinkle room, we go there a lot. If you're under 70 you're chicken of the desert. Of course, I'm way over 70."

"We'll see you there." In the car, Brian Googled the Massive Rooster. "It's in Cathedral City."

The bar was in a strip mall, next to a Mexican takeaway. A rainbow flag fluttered outside, and a poster on the door read "TONIGHT FOR ONE NIGHT ONLY ... Pippa and her Three Performing Drag Queens." The parking lot was half empty. Inside, an elderly woman sat at the piano playing "The Poor People of Paris," while three drag queens whistled along. At a faraway table, they saw Jimmie and his two friends.

Jimmie's eyes twinkled. "What did you think of the Elvis show?"

Brian threw up his hands. "What can you say about an Elvis impersonator firing ping pong balls out of his ass in a restaurant? I mean, that's real talent."

Jimmie agreed. "Where are my manners? I haven't introduced you to my friends. This is Byron 'Bear' Jackson—he played the Tin Man in the touring production of *The Wiz*, and this is Darryl Williamson who played the Cowardly Lion. They're actors."

Darryl smiled. "That was a lifetime ago. When I was a young stud."

Byron laughed. "That's where we met. On stage in *The Wiz*. He caught my heart. I was dating one of the munchkins at the time."

"How romantic." Stéphane's heart fluttered. "And how utterly gay."

To everyone's relief, "The Poor People of Paris" ended. Pippa started in on "Moon River" with the three drag queens singing along.

"You're not really Donna Reed fans, are you?" Jimmie smiled.

"Not really, no. We've just been following the case in the papers. The missing pubic wig. We were there when it was stolen, and we thought we knew who did it, but now we're not so sure. We thought someone at the Donna Reed Fan Club might have some ideas about who was responsible. That's why we came to see you. I suppose I should apologize."

"No, no, no, don't bother yourself. We're as in the dark about the theft as the police are."

After a second Bacardi and Coke and a sing-along of "Send in the Clowns," "Fly Me to the Moon," and "I Left My Heart in San Francisco,"

Brian and Stéphane left the Massive Rooster and drove home. In bed, Stéphane plumped up his pillow. "I hope you don't think that because you bought me dinner, I'm going to have sex with you."

"Nothing was further from my mind. I do love you, though."

Stéphane snored.

19

In Bondage

The following day, after a few laps in the pool, Brian and Stéphane sat at the breakfast table outside in the garden. A pair of mourning doves hopped around on the roof of the house—it was nesting season. A woodpecker tried to sip from the hummingbird feeder but was thwarted by his inability to hover.

"I had fun last night." Brian poured orange juice into a glass. "I thought Darryl was strikingly handsome. Very romantic, him meeting Byron while they were touring in *The Wiz*. Now, there's a story I'd like to hear. And he was dating a munchkin. I'd love to know the mechanics of that relationship. What did you think of Ginger Riverlight? I keep wanting to call him Ginger Spice."

"It was a little bizarre, but fun. He made a great Elvis. The ping pong balls were inspired. Although, I suspect that might be a health violation. Is it legal to fire ping pong balls out of your ass in a restaurant? Especially when that woman had one land in her hair."

Brian laughed. "I know, and her husband was teasing it out with a fork. I hope they threw that fork away. I think if we go there again, we'll take our own knives and forks. Ginger was right when he said his apple fell far from the tree. He's the black sheep of the Riverlight family. That's for sure. Shhh! What's that noise next door?"

Stéphane got to the glory hole first. "The Riverlight's are meditating and chanting."

"*Om Mani Padme Hum, Om Mani Padme Hum, Om Mani Padme Hum, Om Mani Padme Hum.*"

The chant floated away like cartoon musical notes and dissolved into the air. Brian shoved Stéphane aside and peered through the glory hole. "They've stopped chanting. They're dancing now, interpretive dance, bending like trees in a strong wind. Now their leaping like gazelles. They have scarves tied to their wrists. Very Isadora Duncan. I wonder if they've been to see their son in *Priscilla Presley, Queen of the Desert.*"

"I doubt it."

"I wouldn't like my parents to see me firing ping pong balls out of my ass. They never got over finding my pink polyester jumpsuit under the bed back in the 1970s. They went bat shit crazy—my mother had to be sedated. It was the same with my silver platform shoes. I remember my mother saying to me, 'Do you ever see pictures of Jesus Christ wearing platform shoes?' to which I said, "You don't see Jesus Christ wearing a long line bra and stilettos either, but there you are wearing them—without his permission' They threw me out of the house. I was on my own after that."

Back at the breakfast table, Brian buttered a slice of toast. "Is that our doorbell ringing?"

"I'll take a look." Stéphane disappeared, returning a few moments later with Garth.

Brian picked up the jar of marmalade. "Good morning, Garth. Would you like some breakfast while you're here?"

"Those scrambled eggs and hash browns look good."

"Well sit down. Help yourself."

Garth sat down and scooped eggs and hash browns onto a plate.

"How is your wife? We haven't met her yet." Brian had doubts that Garth's wife existed.

"She's coming to my talk in the community hall about 'Living with Herpes.' I assume you'll be there."

Brian coughed. "We'll do our best. What can we do for you this morning?"

"I was walking past Bimbo and Betsy's house. The two women who aren't lesbians. Do you know them?"

"We've spoken a couple of times. I can't say I really know them, though."

"Last evening, I noticed their house was in darkness. They never go out at night. And then this morning, I usually see Betsy walking her Italian greyhounds, Ellen and Rosie, but she wasn't around. Have you heard anything about them going away on vacation?"

"To be honest, we're not that friendly with them. They pretty much keep themselves to themselves. All I know about them is that they used to perform as a double act on stage and they're not lesbians."

"I'd like to check they're alright, but I don't want to go barging in. The MeToo movement and all that. Being a heterosexual man, and a virile specimen full of seed, I don't want them to feel threatened by me poking my nose in their private business. But a couple of nellies like you, that's different. You're not a threat. I thought you might come over to their house with me. I get concerned when women go missing. I used to bang this whore in Vietnam. Can't remember her name now, but one day she just disappeared. So, me being a problem solver, I set out to find her. Turns out she ran away from the brothel and joined the Viet Cong. She went from draining my big hairy nut sacs to shooting American GIs. Quite a change of emphasis."

Brian's jaw dropped. Stéphane zoned out.

After breakfast, the three men walked to Bimbo and Betsy's house— it was half a block away. Stéphane rang the doorbell. The Italian greyhounds barked and scratched at the door. "Can you hear that?"

Brian listened. "I can hear the dogs."

"No, listen. I wish those damn dogs would shut up."

A faint voice inside the house called out, "Help! Help!"

Stéphane looked through the windows. "I can't see anyone."

Garth pulled a leather wallet from his pocket, took something out, and slid it into the keyhole. "I solve problems. That's what I do. I used to mend leaky faucets in the brothels in Vietnam. They used to pay me with pussy." The lock clicked, and the door opened. The two Italian greyhounds jumped around his legs. "I'll wait here. You two go in."

"Hello! Is there anyone home?" Brian stepped into the hallway.

"Help!"

The two men searched each room, then opened the door to a bedroom.

Stéphane stiffened. "Oh my God! I've never seen one of those before. Not in real life. I think I'm going to faint." He slapped his palm to his feverish brow.

"Stéphane, pull yourself together."

"It looks like two little girls lost in a forest."

"Stéphane, it's a vagina. They don't bite. They're not crocodiles."

Stéphane ran outside and joined Garth. "Garth, you'll never guess what I've just seen."

"What?"

"A vagina. I just locked eyes with a vagina. Not a picture of one, a real-life one. It was staring me down. Watching me. Burrowing into my soul. It wanted to speak to me, but it couldn't find the words. I don't speak vagina. I never could get a grasp of the language. I need to sit down. I need a vodka and orange juice."

Betsy was naked and handcuffed to the four corners of her bed in the bedroom. Brian picked up a blanket lying on the floor and threw it over her.

"Thank you." Betsy's voice was hoarse.

On the floor, Bimbo lay unconscious face down. She was wearing a Superman costume. Brian checked her pulse. "She's still alive. What the hell happened here?"

"I'm so embarrassed. Bimbo fell off the dresser. She was leaping to save me from the evil Brainiac who tied me up."

"Ok, that's a lot of words I've never heard in the same sentence before. Where are the keys to the handcuffs?"

"I don't know. Bimbo took them."

Brian called out to Stéphane. "Call for an ambulance."

Betsy became agitated. "Before the ambulance comes, can you remove the appliance? Bimbo will be so embarrassed if they find her wearing it. She'll never forgive me. Please remove it."

"What appliance?"

"The one that Bimbo is wearing."

"I can't see anything. She's lying face down."

"It's underneath her."

"Stéphane peered around the door. "What appliance?"

"It's underneath Bimbo. Stéphane, take a look."

Stéphane lifted Bimbo slightly. "She has two holes cut out of her Superman costume for her breasts. I'm not an expert. Far from it. But her breasts—I'd use the word pendulous—umm—her nipples are pierced. Is that the appliance? The nipple rings. I don't see anything else here. Oh my God, Brian, this dyke is hung like a horse. She's wearing a cock ring. There's another hole cut in her Superman costume for her—umm—considerable appendage."

Betsy snapped. "Just take it off, quickly before the ambulance arrives."

"I'm not removing a lesbian's cock ring."

"We're not lesbians!"

"Well, whatever you identify as, I'm not removing someone's cock ring. That's not in my job description. Anyway, you can't remove a cock ring when there's an erection involved."

Brian gasped. "She has an erection!?"

Betsy was distraught. "She used Viagra. Do something! I don't want anyone to see her like that."

Brian threw up his hands. "She's wearing a Superman costume with cut-outs for her tits and dick, and you're worried about a cock-ring. I would have thought that was the least of your problems."

"Please take the cock ring off her. Please!"

"But she has an erection." Stéphane pleaded.

Betsy sighed. "Get rid of the erection, then remove the cock ring."

Stéphane balked. "There's no way I'm masturbating an unconscious lesbian. Nothing good can come of that. I'm not dancing through that minefield."

Betsy interrupted. "We're not lesbians!"

Brian shrugged. "Then we have a problem."

"Did someone say there was a problem. Because I solve problems. That's what I do." Garth shouted from outside the front door.

Brian shouted back. "Garth, you'd better come in."

Garth appeared in the doorway. "What's going on here?"

"Bimbo's unconscious. She's wearing a cock ring—"

"—A cock-ring! I thought they were lesbians."

"We're not lesbians!" Betsy was getting frustrated.

Brian explained. "Betsy here, who's handcuffed to the bed, wants Bimbo's cock-ring removed before the ambulance arrives. Bimbo, who is lying here unconscious, has an erection and as we all know you can't remove a cock ring when you have an erection. That's the problem."

"That's not a problem. That's easily solved. Somebody needs to jerk her off. Any volunteers?" Garth scanned the bedroom. "No, then I guess I'll have to do it myself."

"I have to talk dirty to her." Betsy interrupted. "She can't orgasm unless I talk dirty to her."

Brian palmed his forehead. "She's unconscious. She can't hear anything. She won't respond."

"But let's try. You give her a hand job and I'll talk dirty. 'Help me Superman, the evil Brainiac has tied me to this bed and I'm a silly little virgin who needs to be tickled between the legs. Where is my Superman? Will he come to save me?"

Garth stroked Bimbo's cock. "This is a first for me, but I think it's working." He rubbed harder. "I can feel some twitching. Oh yes, we're over the hill and on the homestretch."

Eventually, Bimbo shot her load just as the ambulance pulled up outside. As her cock shrunk, Garth skillfully slipped off the cock-ring. He also saw the key, and tossed it to Brian, who undid Betsy's handcuffs. In the nick of time.

Stéphane let the medics in.

"What happened here then?" A wide-eyed medic stifled a laugh.

Brian stepped in. "She was going to a costume party. And she slipped and fell."

Outside, the medic spoke to Stéphane. "I notice they have male genitalia and female breasts. Does this individual identify as male or female? Or genderfluid?"

Stéphane thought for a moment. "I don't know. But I do know one thing, she's definitely not a lesbian."

20
Singing to Plants

The following morning, Stéphane searched through the *Desert Sun* at the breakfast table. "Brian, there's nothing about Donna Reed in the paper this morning. Or the bank robberies."

"I think the whole Donna Reed pubic wig thing has blown over. I suspect the police have decided that the bank robber and the wig snatcher are two different people. And they've got better things to do than waste police time on a silly wig. However, I'm sure they're still after the bank robber. It looks like we were wrong about Jed snatching the wig. Maybe that guy we saw coming out of the Movie Accessories exhibition wearing a fake goatee was just a man wearing a fake goatee. Not Jed at all."

"But that doesn't explain the car incident? Someone tried to run us off the road."

"That was probably just kids. Joyriding."

"Look, we've got a visitor."

Jasper was padding around the pool, the black and white cat from next door. She jumped onto the table, her whiskers twitching—she could smell food. Stéphane petted the cat, who purred loudly. "She's very friendly for an animal that's the reincarnation of Cleopatra. I can't imagine Cleopatra was this friendly. Perhaps Jasper would like some bacon. Would you like some bacon puss?"

"The Riverlights said she was vegan."

"Cats aren't vegan, they're carnivores. Here you are, Jasper, here's a little piece of bacon."

Jasper ate the bacon, licked her lips, purred, then curled up in Stéphane's lap. "We should buy some cat food. Fish, cats eat fish. They don't eat tofu. Have you ever heard of a cat on a plant-based diet? No. Ever seen a lion eating a carrot? No."

"Stéphane, don't get started on pets. You know what I think about pets. Ever since we lived in Chicago, and your tropical fish died of Windex poisoning. Never again. More pets? Not going to happen. Not even a pet rock. Never, ever, forget about it."

The side gate opened, and Margarita and Isabella, the gardeners, walked up the side path carrying honeysuckle plants.

"Don't worry, we're just clearing away the breakfast things. We'll be out of your way." Brian began stacking plates.

"I see you have a cat." Margarita put down the honeysuckle plants and petted the feline. "She's adorable. I love cats. Did you know that cats have three names? The first name is what their owners call them. The second name is what other cats call them. The third name is what they call themselves. What's her name, the name you call her, or is it a boy?"

"Her name is Jasper and she's our neighbors' cat."

"They shouldn't let her out. She could be eaten by coyotes."

"Cats can move pretty fast. They can also climb trees. Something coyotes can't do. How's the acting going?"

"I had a couple of auditions last week. There's an all-female Spanish-language adaption of *Who's Afraid of Virginia Wolf*? I auditioned for Martha."

"An all-female Spanish-language version of *Who's Afraid of Virginia Woolf*? A must see. Did you hear that, Stéphane? They're doing an all-female Spanish-language version of *Who's Afraid of Virginia Woolf*?"

"I definitely want to see that."

"Isabella, tell them about your role in the movie *Nazi Sausages from Outer Space*."

"I play a Nazi bratwurst with a monocle and a speech-impediment."

Brian stifled a giggle. "Another must-see."

Margarita leaned against a palm tree with her thumbs in the waistband of her jeans. "We picked up your plants from the garden center. Martie's here to sing them in."

Brian was confused. "Sing them in! What does 'sing them in' mean?"

"Sometimes, if he likes a customer, Martie sings to the plants as they are planted. Didn't you read *The Secret Life of Plants* by Peter Tompkins and Christopher Bird? Plants like to be sung to. They also like to laugh. Do you know any good plant jokes? You know, like an oak tree, a primrose, and a Cempasúchil walk into a bar—that kind of thing."

Martie appeared carrying two barrel-cactus. He wore an electric-blue sequined ballgown. "Hello, my dears, what a fuss at the White Swallow the other night. They've been warned about that stage before. That wood was rotten. I'm sorry you had to see that. Me going ass over heels is not the prettiest sight. Ruined my Peggy Lee. And the last thing anyone needs at my age, is to have their Peggy Lee ruined. Not my finest moment."

"How are you? You're out of hospital, so you must be better." Brian was pleased to see him. There was something endearing about a 350lb disco ball running a garden center.

"I'm much better, but I'm laying off performing for a while. On stage, of course. I still need to look fabulous offstage." Martie lifted his ballgown. "Do you want to sign my cast? I'm actually thinking of joining the Palm Springs Gay Men's Chorus."

"I'm surprised you haven't joined before."

"Two much drama. There used to be a lot of them, then somebody borrowed somebody else's purse for Halloween and didn't give it back, and half the chorus had a hissy fit and left to form Sing-Along Men. Then they spilt up, half forming Another Gay Men's Chorus and the other half forming the Palm Springs Singers. Then there was more drama with the Palm Springs Gay Men's Chorus, when some of them left to form the

Chorus of Petulant Nellies, who eventually split with three members forming the Drama Queen Chorus, and the rest started Just What the World Needs Another Fucking Gay Men's Chorus. Then four members of the Palm Springs Gay Men's Chorus left in a huff and formed the Fuck This Shit Barber Shop Quartet. But today, I'm going to 'sing in' your plants. Where do you want these barrel cactuses?"

Margarita suggested a spot on the far side of the pool. Martie sprayed his throat and began to sing "Ch'ella mi creda" from Puccini's opera, *La fanciulla del West* ... "*Ch'ella mi creda libero e lontano sopra una nuova via di redenzione! Aspetterà ch'io torni... E passeranno I giorni, E passeranno I giorni, ed io non tornerò... ed io non tornerò ...*"

Margarita planted the barrel cactuses. Jasper, who had finished off the bacon while everyone was talking, sat upright, mesmerized by the music.

Stéphane nudged Brian. "I see the puss likes the singing."

"Cats love Puccini. I read that somewhere."

"What about Andrew Lloyd Webber?"

"Cats hate Andrew Lloyd Webber. Never mention cats and Andrew Lloyd Webber in the same sentence."

21
Tiger Lily at the Doctor's Office

Stéphane thumbed through a copy of *Women's Health* magazine. "Look at this, Brian. I'm thinking of signing up for a Zumba class. What do you think? Can you see me dancing to all those Latin rhythms? Salsa, merengue."

"The answer to that is no, I can't see you dancing to Latin rhythms. Remember the Jane Fonda videotapes back in the 1980s? You put your back out. You were off work for two months and put on 10 lbs. You should do a less strenuous type of exercise, like finger puppetry."

"Finger puppetry? What are you talking about?"

"I read an article about it the other day. It's good for arthritis."

"I don't have arthritis."

"Not now, but you will. Everybody gets arthritis to a degree. Prevention is a good thing."

"Oh, by finger puppetry, you mean this." Stéphane raised his middle finger.

A young woman sitting opposite shielded her daughter's eyes.

"Mr. Dobson." A nurse called out Stéphane's name. "The doctor can see you now."

This was a new doctor for Stéphane—his last doctor resigned the day after Stéphane's previous visit. There had been an incident with a speculum, a tongue depressor, and a reflex hammer. Details of what happened were vague—Stéphane was reticent to talk about it. But the outcome was that Dr. Gandhi retired the next day and moved back to India, and Stéphane had to sleep on his stomach for a week. The new doctor was John O'Donnell, a red-faced Irishman with emerald-green eyes and a liking for black brogues.

Brian sat in the waiting room, reading a copy of *People* magazine and muttering. "Who the hell is Jaden Smith? What, or who, is Jazzy B? Sounds like a new soap detergent. I've never heard of these people. Taylor Swift? Is that someone who can make a suit in seconds? I got left behind somewhere along the way. I'm past my sell-by date." Brian fell silent when he noticed everyone was staring at him.

A man walked into the crowded waiting room with a capuchin monkey wearing a diaper. It sat on his shoulder. The man sat down next to Brian—he noticed Brian leaning away. "Oh, don't worry, this is Tiger Lily my helper monkey. I'm mobility and emotionally impaired. Tiger Lily retrieves things from high shelves, turns the pages of my book, and scratches my itches."

"I'm surprised you're allowed to bring that thing into a doctor's waiting room. Monkeys are known to carry diseases. Leprosy—you can catch all kinds of things from monkeys. And that's a fact."

"It's a helper monkey."

"It's still a monkey."

The monkey jumped onto Brian's shoulder.

"There you are, now she's being friendly."

"Get that thing off me!"

"Oh, she won't hurt you."

"I'm not worried about her hurting me. I'm more worried about what I might do to her. Get that thing off me."

"But I need her. I have mobility and emotional issues."

"You just walked in here on your own two feet. You don't need a monkey. You could try putting things on lower shelves. Emotional issues? Normal people have friends or lovers to care for them. All this

126

'helper animal' nonsense only happens in California. In Chicago, we don't have helper animals, we have something called, 'Grow up and get the fuck on with it.' Now, get this thing off me." Brian called out to the receptionist. "Is this ok, having a monkey in a doctor's waiting room?"

"It's a helper monkey. Some people need emotional support from an animal. We had a ferret in here the other day."

"So, now I'm being discriminated against. He's allowed to bring his monkey in here, but I've had to leave my helper giraffe outside. Why haven't you built a taller waiting room to accommodate *my* idiotic whims and fancies? Anyway, besides that, monkeys should be free and running around the jungle. And monkeys don't wear diapers. Not even in the old Tarzan movies." Brian stood up. The monkey jumped off his shoulder and onto its owner's head, screeching and beating its chest.

"Poor Tiger Lily, look what you've done. You've upset her."

Tiger Lily bit her owner's hand. The old man jumped up and let go of the leash.

"See, I warned you. Excuse me receptionist—excuse me! If you could just get your face out of your phone for a moment. You need to send someone in to give this man a tetanus shot. And rabies."

Tiger Lily jumped onto the receptionist's desk. The woman screamed, then ran and hid in a back room. Then the monkey leapt onto a woman's shoulder. The woman held her breath for a second, then let out an ear-piercing scream. Her husband, a tattooed muscleman, named Manuel, grabbed the monkey by the collar and held it at arm's length. Tiger Lily struggled. Her diaper fell off. At that moment, an elderly woman walked in with her helper dog, a Great Dane called Freddie. Tiger Lily bit Manuel, who dropped her. Tiger Lily then homed in on Freddie. Freddie barked loudly.

A security guard arrived. Tall, handsome, and built like a brick shithouse. Tiger Lily picked a turd up from her diaper and threw it at him. The man jumped backwards, tripped over Freddie, the Great Dane, and fell to the floor. As the guard struggled to his feet, Tiger Lily picked up another turd from her diaper and threw it at Brian. It hit him squarely on the cheek. Brian responded by picking up a chair and throwing it at

Tiger Lily. "I'm going to kill that damn thing. We're all going to get rabies and go mad. We might start—oh, I can't even think about it—our brains may become so ravaged by disease that we start liking Barry Manilow. Oh my god, she's pooping again. That's more ammunition."

Tiger Lily picked up her diaper and threw it at Manuel's four-year-old daughter. It landed on top of the child's head. Furious at this point, Manuel opened a window, picked up the monkey by the collar, and threw it out. The room fell silent.

The monkey's owner leaned out the window. "Tiger Lily, where have you gone? I'm coming. I'm coming."

Brian grinned. "Well, it looks like you're going to have to scratch your own balls from now on."

The man climbed out of the window after his monkey. "Tiger Lily, Tiger Lily." Then he lost balance and fell.

At that moment, Stéphane walked out of the doctor's office and surveyed the chaos. "What happened?"

Brian headed for the door. "Oh nothing. Just a little kerfuffle over a helper monkey. What did the doctor say?"

"He said everything's good. I'm in good health for my age. He did say that I'm due for a colonoscopy."

Brian and Stéphane stepped over the security guard, who was unconscious on the floor after slipping on a monkey turd and hitting his head on the receptionist's desk. Stéphane petted the Great Dane. Outside, the owner of the helper monkey lay on a stretcher being loaded into an ambulance. They overheard a medic. "Apparently, the old guy jumped from a second story window and landed on a monkey. The monkey was alive until the man fell on top of it. Now it's strawberry jelly. What are the chances of that? A man attempts suicide and lands on a monkey. I didn't know we had wild monkeys here in the desert."

"So, Stéphane, when are you having this colonoscopy?"

"In a couple of months."

"I hope we don't have a repeat of the last time you had a colonoscopy. You were supposed to drink that enema liquid."

"I didn't like the taste of it."

"They slid the camera up there and had to pull it out. The colonoscopy was canceled. They discovered what I've known about you for years. You're full of shit."

"Well, that's nice, especially coming from someone with monkey dung on their face."

22
Hong

At the breakfast table, the following morning, Jasper turned up with her sisters, Amethyst and Turquoise, all tempted by the prospect of bacon.

"Stéphane, look what you've started. You never should have given Jasper bacon. Now they're all here. The whole gang. You'll never get rid of them."

Stéphane ignored Brian. "This must be Amethyst who is reincarnated from Catherine the Great. And this must be Turquoise who is reincarnated from Betty Boop."

"Stéphane, Betty Boop wasn't a real person. I didn't know you could be reincarnated from a cartoon character. That means I could be reincarnated from Donald Duck."

"And I could be Snow White."

"No, you're more Cruella de Vil. I can see you herding dalmatians into the kill zone."

Stéphane opened a can of cat food.

"Where did that come from?"

"I bought it yesterday." Stéphane emptied the contents into a bowl. The three cats tucked in, then spread out on the loungers for an after-breakfast snooze.

Brian, Stéphane, and the three cats, froze and held their breath when Heather Riverlight called out from next door. "Jasper! ... Turquoise! ... Amethyst! It's breakfast time! I've got your favorite, tofu scramble!"

When they heard their neighbor's door close, they all breathed freely again. Until.

"Stéphane, is that our doorbell? She's looking for her cats. She'll smell cat food on them. Sniff them to make sure they don't smell of fish."

"I'm not sniffing cat breath."

The doorbell rang again. Stéphane answered it and returned to the garden with Bimbo and Betsy, who aren't lesbians.

"We're here to clear the air and to apologize." Bimbo reddened. "I'm sorry about what happened. I'm deeply embarrassed. Betsy told me about how you removed my appliance."

Stéphane balked. "That wasn't us, that was Garth. He's the problem solver. You should be thanking him. What happened could have happened to anyone. Well, maybe not the Superman costume with the titty-boom-boom cut-outs."

Brian interrupted. "You have absolutely nothing to be ashamed about. You had an accident while sharing a private moment. It could have been us. I mean, Stéphane likes to dress up as a French maid sometimes."

Stéphane's jaw dropped.

"He likes me to call him Mademoiselle Suzie. There's nothing wrong with spicing up your sex life. Sometimes Mademoiselle Suzie needs to be spanked with a whisk. Sometimes Mademoiselle Suzie does a little dance with a feather duster. Why don't you show them how you do it Stéphane? That little dance you do."

Stéphane kicked Brian's leg under the table.

"He's shy. Then there's the thing Stéphane does with the rubber ducks and a stick of butter. So please don't worry, I'm sure you'd do the same thing for us, if—for example—Stéphane got stuck in his cage, or he's too tired to gnaw through the straps."

After Bimbo and Betsy left, Stéphane glared at Brian. "You're so going to pay for that. I'm humiliated. I've never dressed up as a French maid in my life."

"Umm—what about that time in Seattle."

"Once—ok, I dressed up as a French maid once. But that was it. And that was thirty years ago. You make it sound like I do it all the time. Look at me and be honest. Do you really think I could pass as a French maid?"

"No, I suppose not. You'd be quite convincing as a French bag lady, though."

"What a great way to start the day, with you pissing me off."

"The day is going to get far worse."

"Really, why?"

"Tonight, it's Garth's talk on 'Living with Herpes' at the Twilight Manors community hall. After the Betsy and Bimbo incident, I think we're obliged to go. We bonded with him that day. He did solve Betsy and Bimbo's problem. Jerking off a woman and removing her cock ring is a skill. It should be on his resume."

Brian and Stéphane fell silent as a dark cloud of dread passed overhead.

A handful of people gathered outside the Twilight Manors community hall. A woman pointed to a sign on the door. "Tonight's event is canceled due to a burst water main."

"So, there is a God." Brian breathed a sigh of relief. He dreaded cringing through a stream of vulgarities about working girls in Vietnam. Garth had what some people might call "an unfortunate manner."

The crowd dispersed. Brian gasped. "Stéphane, look at that."

Stéphane turned to see Garth and a stunningly beautiful woman walking toward them.

132

Garth waved. "I've just received a phone call to say that my talk has been cancelled. Sorry you all came out for nothing. Maybe we can reschedule it. Brian and Stéphane, I'd like you to meet my wife, Hong."

They both shook hands with the elegantly dressed woman. "We thought we'd go out for dinner. Maybe you could join us."

"We'd love to. Wouldn't we, Stéphane?"

"Yes, that's a great idea."

"How about La Salope Prétentieuse in Rancho Mirage? It's a little pricey, but I think it's worth it. We'll meet you there in an hour."

In the car, Stéphane had second thoughts. "Are you sure you want to be seen in a restaurant with Garth. He can be a little—vulgar. More than a little. All he talks about are solving problems and sex workers in Vietnamese brothels. He doesn't have a restraint button."

"I'm sure he won't be like that with his wife there. He'll be on his best behavior. She's stunning. Was she a model or something? So, refined. Did you see her nails?"

"Alice told me she was a lawyer."

"What does she see in him? He's so uncouth. They're an odd couple."

At the La Salope Prétentieuse restaurant, Brian and Stéphane arrived first and sat at a table in the corner. Garth and Hong came soon afterward. Hong was so beautiful—everyone in the restaurant stared as she walked in and sat down at the table. You could see them mouthing, "Who is she? She must be a celebrity."

Hong touched Brian's hand and smiled sweetly. "I hope you like it here. As a child, I developed a passion for French food. I recommend the *Navarin d'agneau*. It's a lamb stew.

They ordered food and a bottle of red wine.

"I heard that you were a lawyer." Brian smiled.

"Yes, I was a constitutional lawyer in Washington DC. Retired now."

Brian and Stéphane's fears of an evening of vulgarities waned.

"When I arrived from Vietnam after the war, I wanted to give something back to America for welcoming me with open arms. And so,

I studied and studied and studied. I believe it you work hard you can achieve anything. That's the American Dream, isn't it?"

"Stéphane changed the subject. "Where did you buy that dress?"

"This is a Stella McCartney. I've only just discovered her. I bought this in Milan. Garth and I went there for one of our wedding anniversaries." Hong laughed. "But I don't remember which one. And, of course, I adore Vivienne Westwood. I seem to prefer the British designers."

Stéphane and Brian noticed that a hush had fallen over the restaurant as the other diners listened in, trying to find out who this woman was.

"Well, you look stunning." Stéphane smiled. "You have impeccable taste."

"Thank you. Did Garth tell you how we met?"

Brian was nervous. Garth told them they met in a brothel. "No, I don't believe he did."

"I met Garth in Vietnam, many, many years ago. We were destined to meet."

Garth nudged her. "Tell Brian and Stéphane about the moment you fell in love with me."

Hong smiled demurely. "Yes, that's a very fond memory for me. It was the first time he came to see me. He was just another client until I started licking his balls."

A woman on the next table froze, her fork hovering in mid-air.

Garth laughed. "After that I banged the crap out of her, every which way you can think of."

"And some ways you probably haven't thought of yet." Hong laughed.

Garth buttered a roll. His voice boomed around the restaurant. "Oh, these boys are gay, they know all about back door love. They're probably driving up and down the Hershey Highway every night of the week. Hong sometimes slips a finger up there. Don't you, dear? Which one of you two is the girl and which is the boy? Brian looks like he could take nine inches of man meat up his shitter."

Brian's jaw dropped. As did Stéphane's. They fought the urge to run.

Hong clutched her pearls. "Oh yes, I'm sure you know about that. Garth likes me to lick his balls and finger his butthole at the same time. It's his favorite."

It was as if the whole restaurant froze in time.

When dinner was over, Brian and Stéphane couldn't get out fast enough. Outside, they heard everyone in the restaurant give a round of applause at their departure.

Back at home, Brian sank into the sofa. "We must never go to dinner with them again, Stéphane. Ever!"

"Agreed."

23
At the Movies

The following morning, Stéphane added olives to his feta cheese omelet at the breakfast table. He poured himself an iced coffee. "Brian, I'm still cringing about last night. All those 'Housewives of Rancho Mirage' types having dinner with their yoga instructors while their husbands are away on business with their secretaries. Wall to wall face lifts, Botox, and silicone. If I close my eyes, I can still see a room full of dropped jaws. They were horrified and I was mortified."

"You're right, Stéphane, it was awkward to say the least. Who knew that Garth's wife would be as foul-mouthed as he is? One thing I do know, is that we can't go back to La Salope Prétentieuse again—ever! Not that I'd want to at those prices."

"Jasper! Turquoise! Amethyst!" Heather Riverlight called her cats in for breakfast, but they had already eaten. They were stretched out on a lounger next door in Brian and Stéphane's garden.

"Stéphane, you've got to stop feeding those cats. We're already in the Riverlights' bad books over the bidet incident."

"She'll never find out. I can't stand by and watch them eating vegan food. You don't like vegan food, do you Turquoise? No, you don't." Stéphane petted the cat.

Turquoise purred and yawned.

Brian threw up his hands. "I give up. Don't come crying to me when the Riverlights find out you're feeding their cats. I wash my hands of it."

"If they find out, I'll deal with it."

Brian changed the subject. "Anything interesting in the paper today?"

Stéphane picked up the *Desert Sun*. "There's been another bank robbery. This one is in Riverside. This is different. Apparently, the bank manager, Jonathan Mars, was kidnapped at home, and his family was held hostage. They were tied up. One of the hooded robbers stayed with them while the other took Mars to the bank. They targeted three safe deposit boxes and stole $2 million in jewelry.

"So, there are two of them in this gang. Anything about Donna Reed's pubic wig?"

"No. Looks like that's blown over."

"Was there any mail this morning?"

Stéphane dumped a pile of envelopes onto the table. "There's another 20 percent off coupon for Bed, Bath, and Beyond. A couple of bills, one from your dentist. Oh, this looks interesting, the Gloria Swanson Movie Theater is hosting a Vintage Film Festival."

"Any good movies?"

"*Now, Voyager* with Bette Davis. A lot of great movies I've never seen on a big screen. *Auntie Mame*, of course. The Thin Man series ... *Brief Encounter* ... look at this ... *From Here to Eternity* with Burt Lancaster, Montgomery Clift, Deborah Kerr—and Donna Reed. I've never seen it."

"Neither have I. Let's go. When is it on?"

"Tonight."

It was a beautiful evening with a clear sky. Brian and Stéphane joined the crowd lining up to buy tickets outside the Gloria Swanson Movie Theater. They ducked down and hid their faces when they saw Jed and Angelica Fosgrave at the head of the line.

"I can guess what they're here to see." Brian pretended to tie his shoelaces. "Don't let them see us."

Brian and Stéphane waited in the lobby until the Fosgrave's had entered the dark theater showing *From Here to Eternity.* They waited for five minutes, then followed them, keeping their heads down. They settled into two seats near the back. They could see Jed and his grandmother seated near the front. Brian nudged Stéphane, "Look who else is joining them."

"Well, well, well, if it isn't the Donna Reed Fan Club. So, they all know each other. That's interesting."

Stéphane and Brian sank down in their seats. The commercials were playing, including one for La Salope Prétentieus—"Fine dining in the Coachella Valley." Then, three seats away, a phone rang, and a man answered it.

"That's so annoying when people do that. How difficult is it to switch your phone off? It's not nuclear physics." Brian shifted in his seat. He wanted to say something.

The man's voice boomed around the theater. "What do you mean, Geoffrey's taking a year off college and traveling through Europe? Tell him from me, he's finishing college and that's all there is to it. What did Helen say? Helen's done what? So, my son is taking a year off college to become a bum, and my daughter has gone camping. Who with? Who's she gone camping with? Have you tried phoning her? There's no reception—we can't even get in touch with her! Where's this campsite? You don't know! Goddammit Marion, you're supposed to be looking after these kids. You got custody. So, she went with Sarah—who the fuck is Sarah? Talk to Sarah's parents—find out where this campsite is. Tell them to call me at 760 555 0109 that's my work cell number." The man hung up.

The phone rang again. "Steve, go to the office now. Pick up the files and we'll discuss it tomorrow over breakfast."

One minute later, the phone rang again. "I'll meet you at the restaurant tomorrow. Breakfast ... 8 am. That's a bit early for me. OK, I'll be there."

The man hung up. The phone rang again.

Stéphane snapped. "I need the bathroom." Ten minutes later, Stéphane returned.

"Stéphane, you missed all the drama. Our friend here—the jerk with the phone—got a call, went white as a sheet, and ran out. I wonder what that call was about?"

"It was from the guy who runs the Sunnybrooke Camp Site in Steamboat Springs in Colorado. That guy's daughter, Helen, has had a serious accident. Fell off a cliff and is in a coma."

"How do you know this?"

"Well, he announced his phone number and his personal details to everyone in the theater. It was a shame not to use it. Did you know there's a public phone in the lobby? I saw it when we came in. You don't see many public phones these days."

"You phoned him from the lobby and told him his daughter was in a coma?"

"That's exactly what I did. You can't watch a movie when someone is talking loudly on the phone. Now we can watch the movie in peace. It's just starting."

"Stéphane, sometimes I think you're a genius. An idiot savant—but a genius."

After the movie was over, Brian and Stéphane waited until Angelica, Jed, and the Donna Reed Fan Club, left the theater, then they made for the exit.

"So, they all know each other. What's their game? They've been playing us." Brian wondered out loud. "I can smell a rat. Something fishy is going on."

Outside in the lobby, a male couple walking into the theater stopped—one of them called out. "Stéphane, is that you?"

"Oh my god, it's Bill. How are you? What are you doing in Palm Springs?"

"I'm visiting friends. It's been decades. Look, here's my card. Give me a call. I'll be in town for another week. Let's grab lunch. We're late for the movie, so I need to run. *All About Eve,* can't keep Bette Davis waiting."

Bill and his friend disappeared into the labyrinth of the theater.

"Who was that?" Brian thought he knew all of Stéphane's friends.

"That's one of my early boyfriends, back in Fort Wayne. Back when dinosaurs roamed the Earth and Raquel Welch ran around in a loin cloth."

"You haven't mentioned him before."

"When I first met Bill, he had a girlfriend called Daisy. They dated for a couple of years."

"Daisy, that's an old-fashioned name. That's an old woman's name."

"Bill lived on a farm. Daisy was a sheep. His parents gave him Daisy as a pet for his 16th birthday. They had a sheep farm."

"Sorry Stéphane—rewind, I'm getting lost here. Are you saying that he was dating a sheep?"

"Yes. Daisy was his girlfriend. She died. She was struck by lightning. One minute she was grazing in a field, next she was seared lamb chops."

"So, Bill met you when he was on the rebound from a dead sheep. Is this what I'm hearing, Stéphane?"

"Yes, I comforted him when he was grieving."

"Over a dead sheep?"

"Men loving sheep isn't uncommon in Indiana. In fact, it's quite normal. There's nothing much else to do in Indiana. And besides that, Indiana is one of those few states where the sheep are better looking than the people."

Brian was speechless.

24
Jed's RV

The following day at the breakfast table, Stéphane opened the *Desert Sun*. "This is interesting. The police now think that the theft of Donna Reed's pubic wig in Palm Springs is a part of a national Donna Reed-related crime spree. Within the last three weeks there have been Donna Reed memorabilia thefts in twelve other states. The FBI are now investigating."

"I'm beginning to think there may be a Donna Reed Mafia that we don't know about. Or the Donna Reed Fan Club membership could be foot soldiers in a cartel in a Sicilian family. They could be drug mules."

"But Donna Reed was so wholesome and white bread. White everything."

"Have they connected all this to the bank robberies?"

"No."

Brian thought for a moment. "Maybe we should look at Jed again. He lives in the RV in his grandmother's driveway. We need to get inside and take a look. I've got strange feeling about all this."

"Do you really think he's involved in this?"

"Involved in what? That's the problem. I thought from the beginning that this was bigger than one pubic wig being snatched. Something sinister is going on in the murky world of Donna Reed memorabilia collecting, but what is it? And why were the Donna Reed Fan Club members watching a movie with Jed and Angelica Fosgrave? When did they get buddy-buddy?"

"Ok, let's take a look in Jed's RV and get to the bottom of all this."

"What's in that box?" Brian pointed to a package.

"It arrived this morning. It's addressed to you. It's from a Jane Widdicombe in Birmingham, Alabama."

"That's my sister."

"Widdicombe? Did she get married again? She was Jane Johnson last time I saw her."

"She divorced her first husband after he ran off with a girl from the local shoe store. People who sell shoes are not to be trusted. It's a well-known fact that they're amoral, desperately lonely, schizophrenic loners, and suicidal. They believe that the vast emptiness of their pointless lives can be filled by bullying others into buying Crocs. Jane later married a truck driver. I haven't spoken to her in years. I haven't seen her since my mother's funeral. That was a fiasco."

Stéphane laughed. "I was there, remember? Your family wouldn't even speak to me. Apparently, I raped you and introduced you to the twilight world of homosexuality. They looked at me like I was the limb of Satan. Not one member of your family uttered a word to me."

"Well, not quite true. Aunt Mimi called you a pervert and said you would rot in hell for your sodomite ways. Still, you got your own back. Blocking the toilets with torn up newspapers and then dropping laxatives into the wine bottles was a nice touch."

"Well, I was upset. You know what I'm like when I get irritated."

"I certainly do. But your pièce de resistance was squeezing superglue onto the chocolate chip cookies. At the hospital they had to take a layer of skin off Aunt Mimi's lips and her dentures were stuck to her tongue. She was lisping for months."

"Shut her up, though, didn't it? Mission accomplished. So, what's in the package?"

Brian tore at the box. Inside was a ceramic urn containing his mother's ashes and a note. "I've had these for 20 years, now it's your turn." Brian removed the urn and set it down on the breakfast table. "I thought she scattered these years ago."

"I hope you're not going to keep them in the house. I've never understood why people keep the ashes of loved ones around. It gives me the creeps just thinking about it. Remember Bobby in Chicago?"

"How could I forget? He had the ashes of his poodle on the coffee table. Used to crumble up a milk bone and add it to Marlene's ashes every year on her birthday. Then when Bobby died, we mixed his ashes with Marlene's and emptied them into Lake Michigan."

"Not so much emptied as tossed. We went on one of those dinner cruises and you threw the urn over the side."

"What else was I supposed to do? And no, I won't be keeping my mother's ashes in the house. I'll put them in the trunk of the car and next time we're out in the desert, we'll spread them there. It's not like my mother and I were close."

"Don't you have any fond memories of your childhood at all?"

"Let me think. Yes, I do. I remember when my mother washed a pair of her pink panties with my father's white work shirts. And the dye ran. And I remember tying my father's shoelaces together when he was passed out drunk. That's about it. Happy days."

At the Cold Comfort Shake Rattle and Roll Ice Cream Parlor, Brian ordered the Almond Joy shake, and Stéphane, the Key Lime Pistachio cone. Jed was behind the counter. "Hello again, haven't seen you in a while. Any thoughts about selling me that Donna Reed movie still? My offer still stands."

Brian laughed. "No, we got it framed and it's on the wall in our Donna Reed Room."

"You have a Donna Reed room! Are you here in Palm Springs full time, or are you snowbirds?"

"Here all year?"

"Whereabouts in Palm Springs do you live?"

"Oh, we don't live in Palm Springs, we're in Rancho Mirage." Brian lied. Jed was fishing for information.

"I'd like to see this Donna Reed Room sometime. As I told you, my grandmother used to work for her."

"Maybe next time we come in we'll arrange for you and your grandmother to visit and see our collection. We have over 200 items."

Jed's eyes lit up. "I'd like that."

Brian and Stéphane sat on their regular stools in the window, watching the passers-by walking along the tourist strip. A woman with a large floppy flowered hat pushed a screaming toddler in a stroller, and an older child held her hand. She was also pregnant. Her once considerable inner and outer beauty had been sandpapered down by the tantrums of her offspring, leaving her nerves raw. Her husband walked aimlessly behind her, wearing an AC/DC T-shirt and scratching his ass.

Brian sipped his Almond Joy shake. "One of the great perks of being gay is that we can't produce kids. Not without a willing lady friend and a signed legal document. Look at that family there. She's got the kids dumped on her and he's meandering through life thinking about beer and titties."

"Are we that different, Brian? I mean, don't we go through life thinking about cocktails and bulges?"

"Yes, we do. It's a man thing. But we don't have kids at the end of our nocturnal poking."

"Some gay couples do have kids."

Brian threw up his hands. "I have no idea why. I'd rather get my eyeballs pierced. Did it ever cross your mind to have children?"

"No, not once. I would have been a terrible parent. Although, I've heard that kids are quite tasty when fried with onions and a pinch of paprika."

"I've also heard that. We would have been lousy parents. I can't keep a houseplant alive. If I had a child, I'd probably forget to feed it. Or I'd leave it on the bus, and I'd have to go to Lost and Found."

"And it's not like you can change your mind. Once you have a child, you're stuck with it. Even if it turns out to be an obnoxious, selfish, piece of shit—as most of them are. And dumping them in the woods at night to fend for themselves is frowned upon."

"I've heard that to."

Eventually, Jed left the ice cream parlor for lunch. Brian and Stéphane waited twenty minutes, then left and drove to the end of the street where Jed lived with Angelica Fosgrave, his grandmother. Brian and Stéphane waited in the car until Jed left the house and returned to work. Then they slipped through the main gate. In the garden, they edged their way along a wall of red bougainvillea until they reached the RV. It was dilapidated with peeling eggshell blue paint. There, hidden in the shadows, they slipped on their ski masks and gloves. Brian tried the door, but it was locked. "These locks are easy to pick. That's why God created bobby pins."

Inside the RV, the small kitchen had a refrigerator, stovetop, microwave, and oven. Dishes were piled up, and wastebins overflowed with takeaway food boxes, menus, and wrappers. Two bin liners were full of garbage. "Wait a minute." Brian opened a garbage bag. "This isn't garbage, this is money. There must be hundreds of thousands of dollars in here. I think we've found our bank robber. And look at this." Brian lifted the lid of a cardboard box. "We've also found the missing jewels. Make sure you photograph everything."

In the bedroom at the back, the walls were plastered with pictures of Donna Reed. The main lounge area was an office with a desk, computer, and a corkboard containing more images of Donna Reed, including a newspaper ad she appeared in for US Savings Bonds. In addition, two binders lay open on the desk. One contained sheep photographs, and the other had pictures of the Terra Cotta Army of Qin Shi Huang in China.

Stéphane took more photographs, then flicked through the binders. "Jed has diverse interests. Why photographs of the burial ground of Qin Shi Huang, with his terra cotta army? And why sheep?"

"Is this a dating record of your friend Bill in Indiana? Maybe he's running a mail order sheep bride business, and this is the catalog. Look, there's a pretty one here. Look at those legs. I bet your friend Bill would love those four legs wrapped around his neck."

"I should never have told you about Bill and Daisy."

"Baaahhh! Baaahhh!"

"Oh, shut up, Brian."

Stéphane picked up a photograph. "What's this place? It' looks like a warehouse."

"Photograph it."

"I don't get the connection between sheep, Donna Reed, and the Terra Cotta Army of Qin Shi Huang."

"Who said there's a connection?"

"That's true." Stéphane perused the books on the shelf. *Space Aliens in the Bible, JFK Killed by Elvis Presley, Princess Diana and the CIA, The Roswell Cover-Up, History of the Flat Earth Society,* and *Elizabeth Taylor: Woman or Overweight Lizard?* "He's a conspiracy theorist. One of those QAnon people."

Brian heard a noise outside. "Shh!! Stéphane."

Stéphane peered through a crack in the blinds—Angelica Fosgrave was walking to the mailbox. She stopped for a moment and sniffed the air like a hungry wolf. Then she moved on. Brian and Stéphane held their breath until she was back in the house. Then they made their getaway.

25

The Kissing Cousins Diner

The following morning, Stéphane dropped a stack of pictures onto the breakfast table. "I printed up some of the photos I took inside, and outside, Jed's RV. It's quite interesting."

Brian flicked through the pictures. "Why have a binder of sheep photos and another binder of the terra cotta soldiers in China? What's the connection with Donna Reed? Is there one? One thing we haven't considered is that Jed might be insane. It could be that he's just a nut job. He might be a few clowns short of a circus, looney tunes, or as the Australians say, Jed may have a kangaroo loose in the top paddock. And don't forget the conspiracy books on his bookshelf. He probably spends his spare time looking for Hilary's emails, which, as we all know, are buried in a secret room under a cactus in the Mojave Desert."

"But what about the money and jewels?" Stéphane scratched his head. "It's baffling, but somehow all these things are linked together. At least in his mind, they are. Whether they are in the real world, is another matter altogether."

"One thing we know for sure is that he's one of the bank robbers. But who's the other one?"

"His grandmother?"

Brian laughed. "She got tired making us a cup of tea. I don't see her holding up a bank."

"Brian, I'm not entirely convinced that Jed is the bank robber. Bank robbers don't usually work in ice creams parlors."

"Then where did all the money and jewels come from?"

Margarita and Isabella appeared at the side gate. Brian hurriedly gathered up the pictures and hid them under a stack of napkins.

Isabella picked up a photograph that Brian dropped. "I know this building. Look Margarita."

"Isn't that the terra cotta factory on Dillon Road? Yes, look, I recognize the new building next door. And on the other side is the cactus farm. It's not far from where we live in Desert Hot Springs."

"We passed that building driving here this morning."

Stéphane took the photograph. "Do you know the name of this factory?"

"No, I don't know. Do you know the name, Isabella?"

"No, I can't remember, but it's right next to the Prickly Heat Cactus Farm. And a hundred yards from the Kissing Cousins Diner. Excellent food. If you ever go there, ask for Verónica—she's my sister. By the way, I have a gift for you." Isabella reached into her bag and pulled out a DVD. "It's the movie I was telling you about, *Nazi Sausages from Outer Space*. I play a goose-stepping Nazi bratwurst with a monocle."

Stéphane took the DVD. "Oh, we're definitely watching this. Thank you."

"Maybe we'll invite some friends over and watch it together." Brian smiled.

As Brian backed the car out of the garage, Heather Riverlight pulled into hers. She climbed out and lifted two cat cages out of the back seat.

Stéphane wound down the window and called out. "Good morning. Are the cats alright."

"They've been to the vet."

"Are they sick?"

"I thought they were because they're not eating. But when I told the vet they were vegan, he told me that cats need to eat meat and fish to survive. So, we're changing their diet."

"I think that sounds sensible."

On the drive to Desert Hot Springs, Stéphane was elated. "See Brian, I did a good thing. I saved three cats from tofu poisoning. That makes me a superhero in the cat world. Another Catwoman. I should buy myself a little cape. I have superhuman powers, the ability to save cats from terrible diets. I need a tight bodysuit. Something that shows off my muscular frame."

"You don't have a muscular frame. You have the body of a man who died three weeks ago and is rotting in a shallow grave in the woods."

Stéphane ignored him. "But every Batman needs his Robin."

"You've got me."

"No, superhero sidekicks are young and virile, handsome. In fact, everything you're not."

"Thanks a bunch."

"I do love you, Brian, but you're like an old comfy sofa. And sometimes, a man wants to sit on something newer and firmer. Something throbbing with tighter upholstery, strong legs, and balls like grapefruits."

Brian changed the subject. "Are we stopping off for lunch?"

"Let's try the Kissing Cousins Diner."

Brian drove through the desert until they reached Desert Hot Springs. They parked at the back of the Kissing Cousins Diner, in between a rusting brown 1970 Chrysler Newport and a black lowrider with purple velvet upholstery. On the trunk were painted the words "Purple Rain."

The décor had not changed inside the diner since *The Brady Bunch* was shown on the broken TV set that sat on a shelf next to a faded red sombrero. The wallpaper had large yellow and orange circles on a brown background. The restaurant had turned from an American diner to a Mexican diner twenty years before. Still, the décor hadn't changed—it had been added to. In the corners of the room tinsel tufts hung from the ceiling from where the Christmas decorations had been torn down. Brian and Stéphane sat at a table in the window and asked for Verónica. Unlike her reserved, petite sister, Verónica was bouncy and bubbly. Her hair tied up into a tight dancing ponytail, she exuded joy and laughter.

"Your sister Isabella is our gardener in Palm Springs. She said the food here is the best." Brian took the menu.

"She was right, but don't take my word for it. If you have any questions about the menu, call me. Can I get you a drink?"

They both ordered black iced tea.

Brian opened the menu. "It all sounds good. Gorditas de La Villa, Sausage enchiladas, Huevos Rancheros—I'm going with the Avocado Quesadillas."

"Huevos Rancheros for me. I think I'd also like to try these Gorditas de La Villa. No idea what it is. But I'm feeling adventurous."

They ordered their food.

Stéphane stared out the window at the open desert and the mountains in the distance. "I'm assuming this terra cotta factory is nearby. Do we have a plan?"

"Let's play it by ear. I quite like this place, very 1970s."

"There's a restaurant in Fort Wayne like this. It's run by a guy called Rafael Vázquez. I used to go there with Bill."

"Baaahhh! Baaahhh! That Bill?"

"Yes, that one."

"Are you seeing him while he's here in Palm Springs? He gave you his cell number."

"I don't know. Maybe. Anyway, in Fort Wayne, Rafael Vázquez ran a similar diner to this. This was back in the early 1970s. One day I was in there and who should walk in but Florence Henderson."

"No way. Carol Brady. Why would she be in Fort Wayne, Indiana? Come to think of it, why would anybody be in Fort Wayne, Indiana? Did you speak to her?"

"Of course, I asked her what she liked best about being in *The Brady Brunch*."

"What did she say?"

"Nothing, that's when I found out it wasn't Florence Henderson after all. I was so embarrassed. I was getting my TV shows mixed up. I confused *The Brady Bunch* with *The Partridge Family*."

"Easy mistake to make. So, who was it?"

"It was David Cassidy."

"How could you not tell the difference between Florence Henderson and David Cassidy?"

"Quaaludes."

"Well, that explains it."

Verónica brought their food. "You're just in time for Carmen Puta. She is going to sing a song. I think it's by Shakira."

Carmen Puta flew out of the kitchen through the saloon doors and struck a toreador pose. She wore a traditional Mexican long skirt with an off-the-shoulder blouse of brightly colored embroidered flowers, and she cracked a fan. She looked like Divine in *Lust in the Dust*. Puta began to sing with all the passion of a serial killer picking up a fresh victim. She thrust out her ample chest and let rip. "*Para amarte, necesito una razón Y es difícil creer que no exista Una más que este amor Sobra tanto dentro de este corazón Y a pesar de que dicen que los años son sabios Todavía se siente el dolores.*"

Stéphane leaned back in his seat. "I don't know what the words mean, but I like the song."

"I think Puta has a pene." Brian grinned.

"I think you're right."

Verónica refilled their iced tea. "What brings you to Desert Hot Springs?"

151

Brian tore open a packet of sugar. "We're looking for a terra cotta factory. But we don't know where it is."

"Ah that's the Glazier Rock factory. They've just finished building that warehouse next door to it. In one building they make terra cotta, but I don't know what the second building is used for. Juan might be able to tell you. He worked there until recently."

Verónica fetched Juan from the kitchen. "Juan, these are friends of Isabella. They're asking about the Glazier Rock factory. I told them you worked there."

"Only for a few months. That was in the old building. But when they finished building the larger warehouse next door, everyone was fired. They hired all new people. Not local people. The strange thing is that they all arrive in a bus every morning and then get picked up by the bus every night at 5 p.m. Nobody knows where they take them to. And they all look the same, orange jumpsuits. They look like prisoners."

"What did you make at the factory?"

"Roof tiles, but I think they're making something else now. I heard they moved in a lot of new machinery."

"Do you know who owns the factory?"

"No, but I think it's a woman."

26
The Orange Ghosts

Brian and Stéphane passed the Glazier Rock factory as they drove along Dillon Road. There were two armed guards at the gate. Brian drove on and pulled into the parking lot of the cactus farm next door. They could see, only fifty yards away, the entrance to the smaller of the two terra cotta factory buildings. The new building next door was three times the size of the old one.

Brian climbed out of the car. "Let's go cactus shopping."

Inside the cactus farm, Stéphane checked the price tag on a totem pole cactus. "What is there in a terra cotta factory that requires two armed guards on the gate?"

"I don't know, but I'm guessing they're not making roof tiles anymore. There must be something else going on."

"Flowerpots maybe. What about water pipes?"

"Can I help you? My name is Manuel and I'm the owner of the Prickly Heat Cactus Farm. Is there anything special you're looking for?" Manuel smiled, one of those Mexican smiles that lights up the desert. Brian and Stéphane both felt what they called "a flicker in the panties."

Brian composed himself. "No, we're just browsing, trying to get ideas. Our gardeners suggested we come here and write down the names of any cactuses we thought might work in our garden. Do you also own the factory next door?"

"No, no, no. I don't know who owns it, but they're expanding. I think that new building is for storage."

"What are they storing?"

"I don't know but there's a forklift taking boxes from the old building to the new building all day. Look, you can see for yourself." Manuel pointed to the back of the Glazier Rock building. A figure in an orange jumpsuit loaded up a forklift with two six-foot-high boxes.

"Someone told me that the staff were fired recently."

"Yes, every one of them. My brother, Alejandro, worked there. Alejandro!" Manuel called out to his brother. "Tell these guys what happened when you got fired from the factory next door."

"There was no warning. I turned up for my shift and the door was locked. The guards gave me an envelope and said I wasn't working there anymore. No explanation. We were all fired."

"What was in the envelope?" Brian was intrigued. "If you don't mind me asking."

"My wages in cash. In fact, it was more than they owed me. A lot more. So, I didn't complain. None of us did. And then we found out that they employed this other group. They come in a bus in the morning. They get picked up at 5 p.m. and they're driven off up the mountain somewhere. They wear orange jumpsuits. We call them fantasmas naranjas, the orange ghosts."

Brian and Stéphane sank down in their seats outside in the parking lot as a car passed and turned into the Glazier Rock factory. The guards waved them through. The car parked.

Brian gasped. "Well, well, well, can you see what I see?"

"It's Jimmie and Lorna from the Donna Reed Fan Club. What are they doing here? They're talking to the orange ghosts. So, what's the plan? What do we do next?"

"We've got two hours to kill until that bus arrives to pick up the workers. Let's follow them and see where they go. I saw an antique store a little way back. Let's take a look."

The antique store was little more than a tumbledown shack on the side of the road. A sign, dangling from one hinge, read "Art's Artifacts & Curios." Next to the entrance stood a bored-looking cigar store Indian and a rusty horse-driven hay rake.

Stéphane hesitated. "Is this place safe? It's a bit rickety. It looks like it might collapse at any moment."

Inside the store, a small man sat behind a desk. He was in his mid-sixties, wearing an oversize cowboy hat and cowboy boots. He sported a waxed mustache and a patch over one eye. His scrunched-up facial features resembled those of Popeye. He even smoked a cherrywood pipe—it lay in front of him, in an ashtray. The air was thick with the smell of pipe tobacco.

"Good morning gentlemen, my name is Art, and everything in the store is 50% off."

As Brian and Stéphane walked around the store, the floorboards creaked beneath their feet. They weaved through haphazard aisles of midcentury shell chairs, shelves of antique Christmas ornaments, perfume bottles, depression glass, scales and balances, and old photographs.

"That's creepy." Stéphane pointed to a stuffed owl.

"I'm thinking of having you stuffed after you pass away."

Stéphane ignored Brian. "Look, Power Boy books."

Brian looked through the books. "I'm buying these two, *The Mystery of the Missing Leg Warmers* and *The Mystery at the Lesbian Bake-Sale*."

At the counter, Brian paid for the books. Stéphane picked up an heirloom plate. "Look, Brian, it's a scene from *It's a Wonderful Life*. How much is this?"

Art took the plate. "Oh, I'm afraid this has already been sold. I have a standing order for any memorabilia connected to Donna Reed."

"So, there's a collector of Donna Reed material that comes in here."

"Yes. He lives in Palm Springs."

"We probably know him. We're members of the Palm Springs Donna Reed Fan Club."

"Are you really." Art's friendly demeanor changed. "I'm sorry, I'm just about to close." He hustled Brian and Stéphane out of the store.

Standing outside, Brian shrugged. "What was that about? Must have been something I said."

"Maybe it's that Bear Ass cologne you're wearing."

"It's called Bear Ass, that doesn't mean it smells like a bear's ass."

"Well, it smells like somebody's ass. Shh! He's on the phone."

Brian and Stéphane pressed their ears to the door and listened.

"They said they were members of the Palm Springs chapter but they're not. Two guys, one was chubby, and the other was skinny. Asking questions. Didn't get their names. I don't know what they're up to, but they're up to something. I told them I was closing the store. They tried to buy an heirloom plate of *It's a Wonderful Life*—no, of course, I didn't sell it to them."

Stéphane took a photograph of the lopsided sign reading Art's Artifacts & Curios.

Brian parked the car on Dillon Road. "It looks like Art at the antiques store is involved in all this. I wonder who he was talking to."

"I can't believe there are this many people involved in the snatching of a dead celebrity's pubic wig. We're going to feel stupid if we get to the bottom of all this and find out it's got nothing to do with Donna Reed, but something else entirely."

"At least they don't know we're on to them."

"I don't know about that, Brian. Did you hear the guy's phone call? He said, 'two guys, one chubby, one skinny.' They—whoever *they* are— must, at the very least, be suspicious. We have to be very careful."

"Stéphane, you keep a look out for the bus, this old man's taking a nap." Brian leaned back and closed his eyes. He drifted off into dreamland, where he danced naked with Brad Pitt through a bluebell wood. Bluebirds sang in this Disney dream. Deer frolicked in a grassy glade. And rabbits came out of their burrows to watch as Brad Pitt sat on Brian's face. It was his favorite dream.

Stéphane woke Brian at 5:00 p.m. as the bus pulled into the Glazier Rock factory. "It's here, Brian, and they're loading up the workers. There are about twenty-five of them."

When the bus was loaded up, it pulled away. Brian started up the engine. "Can you believe it; the windows are tinted. What are they hiding?"

Brian and Stéphane followed the bus out of Desert Hot Springs and into the high desert. It was getting dark, the sun setting over the mountains. They passed through Yucca Valley and Joshua Tree, then turned off at Twentynine Palms and headed for Flamingo Heights. Brian switched off the lights and drove in the dark, following the taillights on the bus up ahead. Eventually, the bus turned off the main road and drove up a rough track. Brian stopped the car as the bus entered a walled compound.

"There's no way we can get in there. Remember where we are, we need to mark the location of this place on a map." Brian and Stéphane drove back through the high desert, then headed down the mountain to Twilight Manors in Palm Springs.

27

Ground Zero

The following morning at the breakfast table, Brian poured cornflakes into a bowl. Then added almond milk and sliced strawberries. "Let's pick a day and have a potluck launch party for Isabella's *Nazi Sausages from Outer Space*. Let's invite a few people over and watch it by the pool. We've got a screen and a projector. We can have a pool party with a movie."

"That's a great idea. Who should we invite?"

"Alice and Jennie, Garth and Hong, Margarita and Isabella, Bimbo and Betsy, and Martie from the garden center."

"Let's do it. What's that noise next door?"

Brian got to the glory hole first. "They're playing Tibetan finger cymbals. Now they're chanting. Most of the Riverlight clan are there. It must be some pagan diddlypop. You know, where they juggle crystals, get their chakras aligned, and kiss Thor's ass. Or whatever it is that these people do."

"What about that hideous son of theirs, the Benedictine monk. Is he there? What was his name? Doodlebuggery, Assberry, Poodlebuttface?"

"I can't see him. Maybe they're celebrating the dawning of the age of Riverlight with a medley of songs from *Hair*. Oh, I see, it's one of their grandchildren's birthdays. There's a cake. Either it's Nutjob or

Pansypoof, or whatever their names are. They're worshipping the sun rising over the mountains. Now they're singing 'Happy birthday.'"

"Happy birthday, dear Dingleberry, happy birthday to you."

"So, it's Dingleberry's birthday." Brian smiled. "That little mystery is solved."

Sat at the table again, Brian sipped his black iced tea. "Don't you wish our life was as simple as the Riverlights?"

"Sometimes, but that's not us, is it? We're not the sitting around worshipping a rock kind of people. We're more the light the fuse, run like hell, and wait for the explosion kind of people."

"What do you think about Art at the antique store?"

"Well, he wasn't going to sell us that heirloom plate with Donna Reed's face on it. And the phone call—who was he calling? It's got something to do with the Donna Reed Fan Club. He must know about them because he knew we weren't members. We need to find out what Jimmie and Lorna were doing at the Glazier Rock factory. And then there's Jed and Angelica together with them at the movie theater. Looks like they're all in this together. We need to be careful who we speak to. We told Jed we had a roomful of Donna Reed memorabilia, so now we're on their radar."

That night, Brian and Stéphane took a disco nap around 8:00 p.m. At midnight, they drove to Desert Hot Springs and parked the car a hundred yards away from the Glazier Rock factory. At that time of night, Dillon Road was empty. There was a clear night sky, so they didn't need flashlights to guide their way. Instead, they could see by moonlight. Brian and Stéphane slipped on their ski masks and gloves and with a backpack of tools, made their way across the open desert and approached the first factory building from the rear. Stéphane carefully cut through the razor wire.

Brian crouched down. "I don't see any guards. But see over there, there's a light on."

They quickly made their way across open ground, then pressed their backs against the wall of the building. They sidled along until they reached an open window. Coming from inside, they heard the movie *Pretty in Pink* playing on the TV. Annie Potts, as Iona, was saying, "I know I'm old enough to be his mother, but when the Duck laid that kiss on me last night, I swear my thighs just went up in flames! He must practice on melons or something."

Brian peered in the window and nudged Stéphane—it was hard to keep a straight face. Stéphane looked in. Two burly men were sleeping on a sofa, naked, and wrapped in each other's arms. Both bore the same sleeve tattoo with the Marine motto, Semper Fidelis. On the table in front of them was a bottle of poppers, a bag of weed, and a half-empty bottle of Johnny Walker Black Label.

Brian shrugged. "Looks like somebody's been making whoopee on the job."

"I wouldn't mind making whoopee with those two. The one with the beard is hung like a horse. The other one—meh, not so much. Hung like a hamster."

They sidled further along the wall until they found a steel door. It was unlocked. Brian laughed. "These are the worst security guards ever. Why did they hire the Laurel & Hardy Security Co.?"

Inside, they found themselves in a long corridor that ran the length of the building. Brian and Stéphane doubled back to the room with the guards. Stéphane took photographs of the two sleeping lovebirds, then crept inside and stuffed the men's clothes, wallets, and guns into a bin liner. Then they took the keys and locked the two guards in the room.

Further along the corridor, they found another door. It opened into a large office where Stéphane photographed pictures of Donna Reed plastered on the walls. Also, there were photographs of sheep and the Chinese terra cotta army. On a corkboard, there were newspaper cuttings. The *New York Times* headline read, "The Week That Dolly Shook the World."

"Brian, I know what this is. This is Dolly the Sheep. Remember, back in 1997, they cloned a sheep in Scotland."

"Don't tell me they're cloning sheep."

"Not sheep, no. I think they're cloning Donna Reeds."

Brian laughed. "What? That's ridiculous. Why would they clone Donna Reed?"

"Who knows?" Stéphane shrugged.

"It doesn't make any sense."

"That's because you're applying logical thought to conspiracy theorists. Who knows what these people think, or how they think, or even if they think?"

Further along the corridor, another door led into a lab filled with microscopes, test tubes, burettes, pipettes, rubber tubing, beakers, conical flasks, and frothing vials of blue liquid.

"Brian, are we on the set of *The Bride of Frankenstein*? Where's Boris Karloff and Elsa Lanchester? This looks like a 1930s movie set of a laboratory. It's *Dr. Jekyll and Mr. Hyde*. We've walked into an old Hammer horror movie."

Brian beamed. "That's it! They're making a movie here. Obviously, it's top secret. Maybe the cast are holograms of dead celebrities."

"I never thought of that. *The Red Masque of Donna Reed*, *Donna Reed in the Wax Museum*, *Revolt of the Zombie Donna Reeds*. We've stumbled on a movie set for a movie starring a hologram of Donna Reed. How cool is that?"

"But that doesn't account for the bank robberies and theft of Donna Reed memorabilia."

"Maybe that's how they're funding the movie."

"Stéphane, wait, I've got it. I think I know why they're collecting Donna Reed memorabilia. In their addled brains they think that if they collect enough DNA, they can clone Donna Reed."

"But Brian, there's no DNA on a movie poster, or a plate. Certainly not Donna Reed's DNA."

"There might be DNA on a pubic wig."

"That's true. I don't know anything about cloning or DNA, but didn't they clone Dolly with the mammary gland of a sheep and an egg cell from another? Where will they find a mammary gland and an egg cell from Donna Reed? Donna Reed didn't lay eggs, did she? It doesn't make any sense.

Brian shrugged. "Why does it have to make sense? If Jed is involved, we already know that he's a conspiracy theorist. With those people, the more something makes sense, the less they believe it. They're contrarians. If you say something is blue, they'll say that it's red. If you point at a panda, they'll say it's a polar bear. These people are fruit loops. These are the same people who like Barry Manilow."

"I thought we agreed to never mention Barry Manilow again. Anyway, nobody likes Barry Manilow."

"That's true. Maybe people in Fort Wayne, Indiana, like him, where the cultural standards are lower than sea level. But in the civilized world."

"Why are we still talking about Barry Manilow?"

"I don't know. Let's stop talking about him."

"Agreed."

"Let's never mention Barry Manilow's name again."

"I'm on board with that."

They found a museum of Donna Reed memorabilia in glass cabinets in yet another room. Brian examined a collection of Donna Reed lunchboxes. "This must be the biggest collection of Donna Reed memorabilia in the world. Stéphane, look!" Brian pointed to a glass cabinet. "Oh my God! It's Donna Reed's pubic wig. Take a picture."

Stéphane smiled. "I've got it! They're trying to clone Donna Reed from her DNA and her essence. Her smell. Her image. Her very being. They're trying to bring her back. These people think that if you own a pair of Donna Reed's soiled panties, you can pour blue liquid over them, mumble some mumbo-jumbo, and the woman herself will leap back to life for a second coming. Like Jesus. Maybe these people think that Donna Reed *is* Jesus. That it was Donna Reed who gave the Sermon on the Mount, and cured leopards."

"I think you mean lepers."

"Didn't I say lepers?"

"No, you said leopards."

"Whatever!"

"It's a nice theory, but it doesn't answer the question, 'Why?'"

"Well, that's the big mystery of all of this."

On the way out of the first building, they checked in on the two security guards who were still passed out cold, huddled together on a sofa, naked and snoring.

Brian laughed. "This is what happens when you hire two closeted gay Marines as security guards."

"What makes you think they're closeted?"

"Out gay men don't need to get drunk and high to have sex. These two are married to women, you mark my words."

Outside, Brian and Stéphane made their way to the newer building. They unlocked the door with the stolen keys. Inside, they climbed a metal staircase by flashlight. At the top, Brian flicked a light switch. The second building was one massive warehouse. They found themselves standing on a viewing platform. The two men looked out over a terra cotta army of five hundred Donna Reeds, each wearing heels, a three-string pearl necklace, and holding a vacuum cleaner.

A full two minutes passed in silence. Brian and Stéphane were gobsmacked.

"Stéphane, take pictures and let's get out of here. This place is giving me the creeps."

Outside, they made a dash across the desert and climbed through the perimeter fence. When they reached the car, Brian and Stéphane realized that one of the naked guards was chasing them. He stumbled, groggy from the Johnny Walker Black Label and marijuana.

"Brian! Get in the car and start her up."

Brian jumped in while Stéphane popped the trunk, threw in the bin liner of clothes and the bag of tools, took something out, and threw it at the security guard. He reeled, tripped, and fell over. Blood flowed from a gash on his forehead. Stéphane jumped into the car. They removed their ski masks, drove along Dillon Road, and headed back toward Palm Springs.

Brian was flustered. "What happened back there? I saw him go down. What did you do?"

"I threw the urn with your mother's ashes at him. It cracked open on his skull."

"You didn't!?"

"I did. Your mother is at rest now."

"Thank you. I can't think of anything better than scattering my mother's ashes over a naked, drunken, closeted gay Marine, guarding a pottery army of Donna Reeds. It's what she would have wanted."

28

The Evidence

Early the following morning, Stephane pulled the car into the garage. Twenty helium party balloons were squeezed into the back seat. He bought every "Happy Birthday" balloon in the supermarket. Brian and Stéphane wore rubber gloves at the breakfast table while assembling the evidence they had gathered in the Strange Case of Donna Reed's Missing Wig. The two men packed everything neatly into a battered suitcase they had recently found abandoned on the side of the road. Inside, in a pocket, they placed a thumb drive with photographs of Jed's RV, the Glazier Rock factory, the compound of orange ghosts, pictures of members of the Donna Reed Fan Club that Stéphane clandestinely took when they visited them at the Lonely Boner Café, and Art's ramshackle antique store. Also included in a plastic folder was a three-page list of their discoveries, fashioned with cut-up lettering from newspapers and magazines. It began:

"Theft of Donna Reed'S Wig and Bank Robberies SOlved."

Stéphane turned his attention to the possessions of the two security guards. "What are we going to do with the property of the two lovebird Marines?" Stéphane opened a wallet. "James Donaldson, married with three kids by the look of it. Is a member of the Shindig Tittie Bar in Cathedral City. Who's he fooling? He's a Marine. Or ex-Marine. Lives in Riverside."

Brian opened the second wallet. "Antonio Rossi, also married by the look of it. There's a picture here of his wife and two kids. I told you they were married to women. How romantic. It's very *Broke Back Mountain*, isn't it? My heart's a flutter."

"Not very romantic for their wives and kids, though. They can't hide their sexuality forever. It's like wearing a corset, you can squeeze in the fat around the waist, but it just comes out somewhere else. You'd know all about that, Brian, having a fuller figure yourself. I don't know why men like that can't find their balls and come out of the closet."

"Stéphane, that's easy for you to say. You had no choice. It was impossible for you to stay in the closet. Are you kidding? With those limp wrists. Look at you. You're two bra straps away from being female. You must have been the most obvious homosexual in Fort Wayne. Did your mother complain about all your fairy dust clogging up the vacuum cleaner? I think she did."

Stéphane ignored him. "The question is, do we include the guard's possessions in the evidence? I mean, we don't know if they're involved or whether they were just hired to guard the place. They don't look like Donna Reed fans. I can't see two Marines wearing heels and pearls. If we hand in those pictures of them cuddling up naked, it will out them."

Brian shrugged. "I don't think we have a choice. We must hand everything over. We're not detectives, we don't know what's important and what isn't."

"Do you think the guards reported the break-in to the owners?" Stéphane felt a tremor of panic.

"I'm guessing not. If it was me, I'd stay quiet about it. They probably drove home buck naked and picked up more clothes and acted as if nothing happened. If they wanted to keep their jobs, that is."

"We cut a hole in the fence. Somebody's bound to find that. I'm worried we may have tipped them off."

Brian thought for a moment. "Well, we don't have any control over that. All we can do is give all this evidence to the police and get back to our lives. Everything needs to go into evidence. Their wallets, the photos you took of them, their clothes, their guns. Make sure you unload them. If they're outed to their wives, tough shit. Not my problem. Not all gay guys are good guys."

"That's true. Look at John Wayne Gacy and Barry Manilow. They both brought misery to the world, one by murdering thirty-three young men, the other for bringing the song 'Copacabana' into the world. Oh, now it's stuck in my head ... *Her name was Lola, she was a showgirl. With yellow feathers in her hair and a dress cut down to there. She would merengue and do the cha-cha And while she tried to be a star. Tony always tended bar.* ... somebody kill me!"

"Oh, shut up, Stéphane. I thought we agreed we'd never mention— err—that name again."

"What name?"

"Barry Manilow."

"There you said it again."

"Said what?"

"Barry Manilow."

"You're giving me a headache."

Brian took the suitcase to a wooded area near the Twilight Manors tennis courts and hid it in the bushes. When he returned home, Stéphane brought the balloons in from the car. Then he used a burner phone to call the Valley Crime Stoppers and tell them to look in the bushes behind the tennis courts at Puesta De Sol. There they would find information about the bank robberies and the theft of Donna Reed's pubic wig. Then Stéphane tied the burner phone to the balloons and released them. They floated up, up, and away into the morning sky and toward the windmills along the I-10 highway.

"Stéphane, what's the plan for today?"

"I'm getting a haircut and having a beauty day at Hair Be Gone."

"Oh, the sissy place. I prefer Ed's Barber Shop in Cathedral City. Masculine bearded hipsters whose breath smells of tobacco. Dreamy."

"What are you doing while I'm gone?"

"I'm going to catch up with my reading. I'm reading a gay romance novel called *Love in Bali*. It's about Bruce, a young blond physiotherapist, who falls in love with Derek, a young dark-haired anesthetist. The trouble is that Derek is already married to a nurse called Steve, though Steve only has eyes for Rod, an undertaker with a lisp. Derek only finds out about the affair when he smells formaldehyde on Steve's underwear. Bruce, rejected by Derek, starts a relationship with Phil, a straight man who is married to Phyllis. The plot thickens when Phyllis is seduced by Diana after she breaks up with Pauline. Pauline takes revenge by standing in a bucket of cold lard and singing 'Copacabana' by .... "

"Don't say it."

"By Barry Manilow."

"Oh, fuck you."

29
Movie Night

A week later, Stéphane picked up the *Desert Sun* at the breakfast table. On the front page, a headline read, "Hundreds arrested in plot to overthrow US government." He held it up for Brian to see. "Look at this."

"Oh my God! What does it say?"

"The article says that members of a far-right group planned to overthrow the government with a terra cotta army of exploding Donna Reeds."

"As we suspected."

"They believed that if they collected enough mementos of Donna Reed, they could clone her."

"Again, as we suspected."

"They've arrested people all over the country and are charging them with sedition and treason. Apparently, the plot was hatched by the National Donna Reed Fan Club after it was taken over by QAnon types, Flat Earthers, and other credulous fools."

"So how were they going to overthrow the government?"

"They were organizing a march of Donna Reeds on Washington. This vast army of pottery housewives were programmed to walk into federal buildings and then explode. At least, that's what they planned to do. Obviously, it couldn't work. It's a stupid idea."

"But why were they doing it? That's what I don't understand. What were they trying to achieve?"

"Apparently, these Donna Reed nuts thought that life in America was better in the good old days—when men were men, and women were in the kitchen whipping up a delicious meatloaf and green bean casserole. They believe that Donna Reed's world, depicted in her TV series, was far superior and we should get back to the values of the late-1950s and early 1960s."

"You mean back when homosexuals were imprisoned and there were White Only drinking fountains."

"Yep, those were the good old days. And the Cuban Missile Crisis, conical bras, poodle skirts, sock hops, and hula hoops."

"And this was happening all over the country?"

"Yes. There were twenty-eight chapters of the Donna Reed Fan Club, and they were all robbing banks to pay for this terra cotta army. The Philadelphia chapter had a warehouse with over 1,000 terra cotta Donna Reeds in it, all ready to go and vacuum up society's filth."

"And some gay individuals were involved in this madness. Sad, but not entirely unexpected. If there's one thing I've learned in my life, it's that gay folk can be just as stupid as anyone else."

"You got that right."

"Was there a ringleader?"

Stéphane laughed. "You won't believe this, but the mastermind of all this is Angelica Fosgrave. They've arrested her. That nice little old lady who thought we were morons?"

Brian shrugged. "Well, she certainly fooled us. We didn't suspect her, so I guess she was right. We are morons."

"Ethel Morons."

Later that day, Brian erected the projector and screen near the pool. Stéphane spent the afternoon in the kitchen making vegetarian lasagna and salads. Vegetarian because the Riverlights from next door were coming. This was the first time Brian and Stéphane had entertained since moving to Palm Springs. Their dinner parties in Chicago were legendary, spoken of in hushed tones, especially when they hosted a potluck Games Night, and a drag queen burst into flames halfway through a contentious game of Monopoly.

As the sun set over the mountains, Margarita and Isabella arrived first with a tray of chicken tamales.

"Isabella made these. My cooking skills are very limited. I can make toast and spread peanut butter on it. That's about it. I could burn salad."

Stéphane laughed. "That's like Brian. Can't even boil an egg."

"That's true. I admit it." Brian opened a bottle of wine.

Margarita ran her fingers through her long curly hair. "Did you read about the Glazier Rock factory in the paper this morning? That's the place you were asking about in Desert Hot Springs. You had a photograph."

"Yes." Brian bristled. "In the end we never went there. Stéphane wanted to look at roof tiles, but we got distracted. Now, I guess, we'll never get there. I assume it's closed down, with all this scandal."

"We drove past on the way here and there are police everywhere. The whole place is sealed off. They've also arrested the guy who ran Art's Artifacts & Curios. There's a rumor he made bombs for these stupid pottery soldiers."

"Why, what's happened?" Stéphane appeared from the kitchen.

"It's all over the papers. There was a secret plot to overthrow the government." Margarita dropped the tamales onto the buffet table.

"Really!" Stéphane feigned ignorance.

"I meant to tell you about it this morning." Brian leaned back against the sink. "I read this article this morning in the *Desert Sun*. Some right-wing looney group tried to take over the government. They built an army of exploding terra cotta Donna Reeds. They were going to march on Washington and bomb federal buildings. It was some cockamamie plot dreamt up by some nut job in Palm Springs, a woman—I can't remember her name."

"Wow, I didn't know anything about this."

"Just another bunch of fools."

Isabella wandered into the garden. "I've never been to a pool party movie night. Specially to watch a movie that I'm in."

Brian joined her. "Look, a shooting star." He pointed at a streak in the sky.

"Ah yes. That's what the movie is about, traveling through space. It's about finding home. Finding a place to belong. And we all want that, don't we, Brian?"

"Yes, I suppose we do. That's something we all have in common."

"I found home when I met Margarita. She was the other half of my amulet."

"And Stéphane is the other half of mine."

Next to arrive were Jennie and Alice with their chihuahua Mitzi. They brought a tray of deviled eggs. They were followed by Betsy and Bimbo, Garth and Hong, Erik and Heather Riverlight, and lastly, Martie in a stunning ballgown. "I made this German chocolate cake with my own dainty little fingers." He looked at his fat porky hands.

The partygoers settled around outside in chairs and on loungers. Betsy and Bimbo sat on the pool's edge and dangled their legs in the cool water. The chicken tamales were a hit, also the German chocolate cake. Brian bit into a second slice. "Martie, this is delicious."

"I love chocolate and cherries." Alice took another bite from her slice.

Martie smiled. "I'm glad you like the cake. I made it myself from scratch and used marijuana that I grew in my own garden."

Jennie choked. "Oh, I've eaten two slices. Oops!"

Heather Riverlight laughed. "That's funny because we put magic mushrooms in the vegan quiche we brought."

"Oh dear, I've just eaten a slice of that." Hong giggled.

Margarita relaxed as the marijuana kicked in. "Can you believe those idiots thought they could clone Donna Reeds? What were they thinking?"

Martie laughed. "I think they picked the wrong TV star. Their silly little plot might have worked if they chose someone else. What about an army of Barbara Edens from *I Dream of Jeannie* or Elizabeth Montgomery from *Bewitched*. That would have worked."

Heather Riverlight giggled. "Or Lucille Ball."

"Or Mr. Ed." Garth laughed at his own joke.

Brian jumped to his feet. "So, who wants to see *Nazi Sausages from Outer Space?* Isabella, tell us what it's about. In fact, give us a running commentary."

Isabella laughed. "The movie is about a race of Nazi sausages that fly across the universe from Planet Knockwurst, after they realize their planet is being eaten by zombies. The Nazi sausages are ruled over by a fat leberkäse called Ada Hitler. She wears caftans and espadrilles. She looks like a cross between Mama Cass and Placido Domingo. To save their own skins, the Nazi sausages escape on a spaceship and eventually land on Earth."

As the movie progressed, Isabella continued her running commentary. "See here, they land on Planet Earth, somewhere near Portland, Oregon. That's me wearing a monocle, descending from the spaceship. The plan is for the Nazi sausages to insert themselves into human bodies and the humans become Third Reich robots."

Jennie wondered. "So how do they insert themselves into humans?"

On the screen, a Broadway dancer/actor/stripper/hooker/waiter leaves a theater and heads home to his studio apartment in New York City. He was appearing in *Phantom of the Opera*. Once home, he showers, takes a shot of gin, and climbs into bed. Hungry but too tired to eat."

Stephane giggled. "Nice ass."

"Well, I'm a lesbian and even I can tell that's a nice man-ass." Margarita took another bite of the Riverlights vegan mushroom quiche.

Martie laid back on a lounger. "Where's the Nazi sausage. Where's Isabella? Oh, there she is climbing onto the bed. Oh my god, no! Is that sausage going where I think it's going? That's an enormous sausage, isn't it?"

Isabella continued. "Yes, I crawl up the dancer's ring of fire while he's sleeping. Of course, it's computer generated, like that scene in *Trainspotting*, where Renton dives into the toilet. Nobody can take a human sized sausage up their ass."

Brian clenched. As did Stéphane.

Isabella continued. "This is a flashback. Back to the Nazi rallies on Planet Knockwurst."

In the movie, Ada Hitler stood behind a lectern and spoke. "Ve attempted to fight ze onslaught uff zombies, komingkt here to planet Knockwurst to destroy our vay uff life. Sadly, mein fellow sausages, ve haf failed. Zerefore ve must fly across ze galaxy to find a new home. Ve vill take possession uff new aschholes undt make zem ours. Efery asschole on Planet Earzz vill belong to us."

Brian flashed Stéphane a look. They were both reminded of the terra cotta army of Donna Reeds. Brian wondered if this was how Adolf Hitler rose to power by shoving sausages into the assholes of blond-haired, blue-eyed, Aryan youth. It was an intriguing thought.

Stéphane felt the swirling effects of the mushroom quiche. As did all the guests at the party. Hong wondered why the jasmine flowers were winking at her.

Isabella continued. "Now my sausage is deep inside the dancer/actor/stripper/hooker/waiter, and I inject him with Nazi juice. He then turns into a robot."

Brian giggled. "This is more like a colonoscopy than a movie."

"Does he know he's got a sausage up his ass?" Stéphane was losing the plot.

"Not until later in the year when he's cast in *Hamilton*." Isabella continued. "On his first night in *Hamilton* he feels something moving in his asshole. That's because I start to wriggle inside of him which interferes with his performance. He orgasms on stage halfway through

'Guns & Ships.' Eventually, he sees a doctor and I'm removed from his asshole."

Garth watched two stars dance the polka in the night sky.

At movies end, Ada Hitler is destroyed by a new drug that shrivels Nazi sausages. Then, in the final scene, the Broadway dancer/actor/stripper/hooker/waiter—now free from his pulsating ass-sausage—tap dances across the stage naked, his genitals bouncing around like a rubber faucet. And then he freezes in midair."

After the movie ended, there was a round of applause, and the partygoers toasted Isabella with a glass of wine. Then they all zoned out.

Brian daydreamed. "You know, Stéphane—you know who would have been great in the role of Ada Hitler?"

"Don't say Donna Reed."

"No, not Donna Reed. Barry Manilow."

Stephane sighed and stared up at the night sky, at the stars twinkling. "Fuck you, Brian. Fuck you with a huge Nazi sausage—up where it hurts."

Just then, twittering Disney bluebirds danced around their heads singing. *"Her name was Lola, she was a showgirl. With yellow feathers in her hair and a dress cut down to there. She would merengue and do the cha-cha. And while she tried to be a star Tony always tended bar Across the crowded floor, they worked from eight til four. They were young and they had each other. Who could ask for more? At the copa Copacabana—"*

Then everyone at the party sang along, even Mitzi, the chihuahua. *"His name was Rico. He wore a diamond. He was escorted to his chair, he saw Lola dancing there. And when she finished, he called her over ... "*

It was the best pool party EVER.

About The Author

For three decades, St Sukie de la Croix, 70, has been a social commentator and researcher on Chicago's LGBT history. He has published oral-history interviews; lectured; conducted historical tours; documented LGBT life through columns, photographs, humor features, and fiction; and written the book Chicago Whispers (University of Wisconsin Press, 2012) on local LGBT history. St Sukie de la Croix, the man the *Chicago Sun-Times* described as "the gay Studs Terkel," came to Chicago from his native Bath, England, in 1991. He has had columns in local publications or online news and entertainment sources such as *Chicago Free Press*, *Gay Chicago*, *Nightlines/Nightspots*, *Outlines*, *Blacklines*, *Windy City Times*, and *GoPride*.com, as well as numerous others outside the city. In 2008 he was a historical consultant and an on-screen interviewee for the WTTW television documentary *Out & Proud in Chicago*. In 2005 and 2006, he had two of his plays, *A White Light in God's Choir* and *Two Weeks in a Bus Station with an Iguana*, performed by Chicago's Irreverence Dance & Theatre Company. A popular and engaging lecturer, he has spoken at various venues from Chubb Insurance to Boeing and from Horizons Gay Youth Services to the Chicago Area Gay and Lesbian Chamber of Commerce. His crowning achievement came in 2012 when the University of Wisconsin published his in-depth, vibrant record of LGBT Chicagoans, *Chicago Whispers: A History of LGBT Chicago Before Stonewall*. With a foreword by noted historian John D'Emilio, the book received glowing reviews and cemented de la Croix's deserved position as a top-ranking historian and leader. In 2012 de la Croix was inducted into the Chicago LGBT Hall of Fame. Two years later, he moved to Palm Springs, California, and in 2017 published *The Blue Spong and the Flight from Mediocrity*, a novel set in 1924 Chicago, followed by *The Orange Spong and Storytelling at the Vamp Art Café* in 2020. In 2018 he published *The Memoir of a Groucho Marxist*, a work about growing up Gay in Great Britain, and in 2019, *Out of the Underground: Homosexuals, the Radical Press and the Rise and Fall of the Gay Liberation Front*. Also, in 2019 he published *St Sukie's Strange Garden of Woodland Creatures* with celebrated illustrator Roy Alton Wald. In 2019, St Sukie de la Croix and Owen Keehnen launched their Tell Me About It Project, which led to the 2019 publication of *Tell Me About It*, *Tell Me About It 2*, and in 2020, *Tell Me About It 3*. In 2020, St Sukie published, *The Orange Spong and Storytelling at the Vamp-Arts Café*, the second book in the popular *Spong Series*. St Sukie continued his LGBTQ Chicago history series in 2021 with the publication of *Chicago After Stonewall: A History of LGBTQ Chicago from Gay Lib to Gay Life*, picking up the narrative of the Chicago LGBTQ rights movement from where his first history book, *Chicago Whispers*, left off. It follows the movement from the day after the Stonewall Riots in New York through to the formation of the Chicago Gay Liberation Front to the publication of Chicago's first regular gay newspaper, *Gay Life*. In 2021, St Sukie, published *Twilight Manors in Palm Springs God's Waiting Room*, a hilarious comic novel. His latest books are, *Last Call Chicago: A History of 1001 LGBTQ-Friendly Taverns, Haunts & Hangouts*, with author Rick Karlin, and *Twilight Manors in Palm Springs: The Strange Case of Donna Reed's Missing Wig*, book two in the wacky series following the adventures of Brian and Stéphane as they continue to bring madness and mayhem to Palm Springs.

CPSIA information can be obtained
at www.ICGtesting.com
Printed in the USA
LVHW100318110423
743974LV00003B/510

9 781955 826211